Percy's Plan

by
Paul Jansen

A text in faire English for modern ears,
a tale of a time whence travelers appear,
twixt chambers and courtyard, or hither to meet,
some longing, some laughing, some leery, some sweet.

Prologue

Emerland was a large commonwealth empire. It was bordered in the east by the Tayler River and around the outlying regions by smaller established territories and governances. Its culture was comprised of five distinct parts. There was the Anover Region in the north-east, populated primarily by a variety of titled ladies and lords, aristocrats, wealthy traders and the like; The Royal Court district in the north-west where the royals and the most wealthy classes were, The Brolen Region in the south-west where many peasant farmers and trades people lived, and the Broadmoor Region in the south-east which was a lower class district where could be found sailors and travelers, as well as those who had recently immigrated and much of the criminal element. Between the south-west and the south-east, bordering the northern regions was a vast forest called the Berkshires. This forest was comprised of a mix of the population including those who had means and money but wished to live a life closer to nature and of more freedoms than the social structures of the court generally adhered to. Many maintained connections to the courts society as a source of income in different capacities, and often made use of barter which was commonly practiced and accessible in the Berkshires. There were often people passing through the forest on a regular basis as per occasion -travelers and thieves among them.

There were three main variations of language that developed in Emerland. In the north, a literate and formal style of speech held sway, In the Berkshires many favored a more lyrical and poetic variant, and in the south there was a simplified language of some of the peasant class and a mixture of other dialects. Often though, people would alternate between the speech of different regions depending on their education and the social situation they were in. Books were just beginning to become more accessible and affordable due to the advent of the printing press, though the upper classes were most often better educated and well read. Many people who were raised in the southern regions went to work as servants and maids, shopkeepers and the like in the north. One such person was a young maidservant named Emily.

PART ONE - INTO THE FOREST

CHAPTER 1

A young maidservant named Emily stood in a small dimly lit
kitchen. She skewered one by one, three cuttings of meat and two
slices of fish which were being smoked on a level platform at the
back of a large cast iron stove, then placed them on a wooden
cutting board. Emily sprinkled them with nutmeg and ginger and
pounded them with a wooden tenderizer. She then brought over a
cask and removing the top splashed all the pieces lightly over with
wine. She went to the stove and threw some chopped salary and
sprouts into a pan where potato slices were frying, then cut a
dollop of butter and dashed it into a second pan to heat. After a
quick glance behind her, she grabbed a piece of fried potato from
the pan with her fingers and ate it.

    Emily pondered something for a moment then she turned to sit
at a bench table and wait for the second pan to heat. She rested her
chin in her hands. Her thoughtful eyes wandered -as they often
did- from the mundane aspects of her position. Straightening up a
bit in her seat, she began to sing quietly:

What does a girl do for pleasure?
oh, tell me, what can she do?
when there is no time away, no friends or games,
just sing as the work's gotten through,
potatoes, pock marked and horn limbed,
I scrape them to their knoll,
nuts and grains, apple and raisins, mix them in a bowl,
celery and sprouts, wash them all out,
chop, chop, their thin filament strands,
the hare and the quail, the trout by avail,
come again to the frying pan.

Emily sighed, then spoke:

"'Tis my song to pass the time. An ode to my productiveness. The
work does have its benefit: a stolen one, from pan to throat

-meager celebrant. But I will not let the short order make me peckish, for that taste is not to my liking for long. Sometimes the heat of the stove can make me see stars. I would bid one to fall 'pon my head, if only for a change, and knock me silly; though when I shake it off, I'm sure 'twould be a roasting pot or the like. Alas, in this new place of employ, I still am assessing *the this*, and *the that*... Marry though, I could knock something unhooked -as an accident- and spend the day in bed perhaps; though that would be an iffy perhaps. Hark. I hear the headmistress."

The headmistress came in and looked at the stove. "The cuts girl. The pan is more than ready."

Emily darted over to the stove and jabbed the pieces of meat and fish, dropping them into the pan to fry. She came back to the table as the headmistress sat on the other side of her.

The lady sighed. "'Tis a grey afternoon. Give me some entertain. Do you have a story for me?"

Emily looked at her. "What? Something simple, as the day?" "Any," said the headmistress, "But as we have ear to our privacy, why not make it one suited to't, and not of such common sort. Something with a bit of scandal, if you may, and I will keep it mum to any other effect but as a stimulant to the lagging hour."

"And you. Wilt thou tell one?"

"I will."

Emily shifted in her seat and thinking for a moment, made a hesitant face at something that came to her, then glanced once at the headmistress who gave her a reassuring smile.

"Go on," the older woman said.

"Very well," said Emily. "Once in my previous employ, whilst I was bathing in my maid's chamber, the mister had entered without announcement as he was sometimes apt to do. Upon seeing me he apologized, but stood there at his spot. 'Sir,' I said, feeling this tidbit enough to underline his lack of good curtailing reflexes, but he continued to stand there. 'Sir,' I said again more pointedly at which he answered me, 'Yes Madame.'

The head mistress looked at her with wide eyed surprise. "He didn't?"

"He did. And so I took kinder leeway with him and asked him to bring me a towel, which he did as though at my beck and call. Hence, I told him he could leave. 'Must I,' he asked? 'Why. What else wouldst thou do for me?' I asked. 'Anything,' he replied. Finding a cruel sort of fascination in this feverish bid of servitude, I did note in it, a desire for some recompense; Thus, I asked him to kiss my hand, which he did -then waited expectantly. 'Now kiss my foot as well that it feel appreciated,' I said. I raised it out to him from the bath and he took it and laid kisses from heel to toe as though it were the tastiest morsel. His complexion was flushed and hot, thence he let out a moan then dropped his head and in an instant, left the room. From there on, it was as ignominious adventitious. He considered himself a pious man and I having instigated his impropriety, was asked to leave the next day with curt distaste."

The headmistress put her hand to her mouth. "Astonishing."

"I have no word for it," said Emily. She looked to the headmistress. "And thee..."

The lady looked at Emily with caution. "You be mum of it as well."

Emily nodded. "On my word."

"This day had brought to me, a remembrance that has stayed with me. It had desired some ears as much as an even exchange and now it has. 'Twas upon this day into night, of a many years past that I delivered a child in this household to a maid who appeared at the doorstep. I having heard a knock 'pon the door that night went to answer it and there stood Jane Harlow. She was a chamber maid who worked here with me for some time. She asked to speak to the earl and I let her in. I remember he had come down and taken her into private to speak and was upset with her. I saw that she was in some physical distress, and I did from experience, have an inkling why. Was soon after that I heard her cry out and the earl shouted for me. Whence I entered the sitting room, she was in pains of labor, so I laid blankets of the floor and set her down on them to give birth. 'Twas a difficult labor and after it, her face was so pale and beaded in sweat I thought she might not live to see the child. Having swaddled the babe, I was taken at arm outside by the earl himself and ordered to bring it immediately by carriage to an orphanage. I thought it only proper to give the child a name first, so I called her Anne. Whence I returned, Miss Harlow was gone. I still'nt feel right about doing what I did but it's not so uncommon a practice, and therewith, I felt at the mercy of my employ, or the streets. Now I feel the pangs of that decision."

"My goodness," said Emily.

"Now, ask me no more of't," said the headmistress. "I tell you this with some measure of vagueness that you might come to conclusions on your own and be heedful, for you are a pretty girl, and the earl has taken some notice of you by that measure."

"I will than missus. My thanks."

The earl had finished up his lunch and gone to the garden, while Emily was cleaning a chamber room upstairs. She stopped her dusting and looked up into the bureau mirror to reassure herself that she did not yet look so much like a maidservant that she might come to find a better life. But what? Just then, the headmistress entered the room.

"Come girl. Have ye not finished that yet? You are scores younger than I, yet my work speeds ahead."

Emily went back to her work. "Sorry miss. I had a thought."

The headmistress chided, "For us, thoughts make for dust, not remove it. Our work is work of the hands, not of the mind."

Emily nodded to her "Yes." The headmistress went to the other side of the room and assisted with finishing up the cleaning.

"Now come. There is something else." Emily followed the headmistress who led her out into the hall. As they walked down the hallway, she looked at a portrait on the wall of an unfamiliar woman with a frilled dress on. She wondered if it was the earl's wife who had died some years ago. He had not re-married again. The headmistress took Emily into the earl's bedchamber.
They both stood there a moment. The woman walked over to the window and looked down to the garden. She turned back to Emily. "Make clean of the earl's chamber whilst he is about the garden. If he comes to't, continue about your work, lest he ask you to take leave."

Emily nodded and said under her breath "As a prig to his loins."

The headmistress turned and chided her, "Tsssst. None of that. You promised."

Emily looked down. "I am sorry. We being alone." The headmistress gave her a look then left. Emily stood for a moment in thought. She walked to the book shelf and looked at the book spines with curiosity to see what the earl would read. She then walked over to the unmade bed and sat down upon it. Emily hoped that she might be sent on an errand somewhere that day, which was her favorite sort of work. There was a runner in the hallway upstairs that prevented her from hearing the earl's approach when he came to the door a moment later. He had already opened it by the time she got up from the bed. The earl stepped inside then stopped and looked at her with a questioning furrowed brow.

"What is thou purpose girl?"

"Sorry sir. I was considering where to begin of my work."

"Doth take such consideration?"

Emily looked down with a submissive bow of her head. "I fear, as your headmistress has pointed out, my thoughts sometimes overtake the occupation and should be kept to a minimum."

He closed the door and turned to her again.

"Your thoughts are of your occupation though?"

"Yes sir," Emily answered.

The earl looked at her for a moment. "I hear a quaver in your answer; your eyes look down. When thou were sitting 'pon the bed, did thee think of the bed and its usage or just of its making?"

"Its usage sir is obvious to anyone of experience."

The earl raised his eyes a bit. "Experience.- of sleeping? Why, a babe has it." He looked at her closely. "No than. Of which experience do you speak?"

Emily fidgeted and continued to look away from him. "Please sir. I was just giving answer; not descript."

The earl stepped closer to her. "Do you know of what you answer? Maybe you are as a babe; one who wonders. I could show thee. Your figure me thinks is more suited to it than sweeping. Your eye has more in it then where to dust. Your clothes could be put to better usage on the floor. Let me slip them off for you."

Emily clenched her nails into her palm as the earl began to reach for the buttons of her top.

"No," she said, pulling away.

"Come. Be a good girl." The earl held her to him more forcefully and Emily knew she must think fast.

"I will lay with thee if you grant me one thing."

He eased his grip on her. "What be it?" he said with an arrogant tone of allowance.

"I wish to be called by another name."

He looked at her perplexed. "But why?"

"That I might make distinct, one; from the other. Maid - from mistress."

"By what name than?" he said mundanely.

"Anne." Emily's knee went up with force and the earl felt the blow between his legs and crumpled to the floor. She darted from the room and as she reached the bottom of the stairs, she heard the earl who had crawled out onto the landing, pull himself up on the banister.

"Haughty fool of a girl. Thou hast pains to suffer for such an affront. I will see to it!" he shouted down to her.

After leaving the earl's house, Emily had gone to the shops district in Anover. She walked around the streets for a bit, then decided she needed to get out of her uniform. She found a pawn shop and went inside for some clothes. Emily surmised what a terrible predicament she was in, realizing she had no money on her person as well. The woman in the pawn shop said she would trade her a cheap cotton dress for her maid's uniform though, so she did, then left to walk about the streets again. When Emily rounded a corner, she suddenly noticed two rough and purposeful looking men. One was asking questions of someone and the other stood and watched passers-by. As he looked in her direction she ducked down and dusted off her shoe.

"Do they come for me? Is it I? The woods are at your heal. Think no more. Turn and you'll be there in an instant." She looked again and saw them approaching at a distance. The one was looking directly to where she was. "Yes. 'Tis I." Emily rose up and crossed the street to where the Berkshire forest bordered the Anover region. Without looking back she ducked into the woods and began to run into the covering trees.

CHAPTER 2

In another part of the Berkshire forest, a young man was wandering. He was dressed in an embroidered vest, a cotton shirt, beige pants and travelling boots. He stopped every once in a while to listen to some sound or inspect a plant, then carried on and spoke:

"'Tis here I come to thrive. Where trees and rivulets are the art and architecture, where a breeze blows my mind of fickle ornament and stirs its depths with contemplation, where time has no expectation of I, and I no hurry for it, and Aves mark the clock and tune. 'Mongst society, I find an eager tongue one moment, a purposeful step the next, a trip to entertain, a sweetheart here who smiles; fellows there of business or jest to tarry with. 'Tis all well and good, but a time there is when spirit aches for a more contemplative understanding of its nature, and so furnished to the purpose is a wondrous place as this, as I have known since I on two feet. Away then, to its faceted nooks and glades."
Daniel jumped over some rocks across a stream and went further into the woods. Soon afterwards, he entered a clearing and as he was crossing it, two men came out from the trees on the other side. They approached him.

"Ho there. Sirrah. A word of yee."

Daniel approached them. "Out here? Doth purpose find its place so far from other men or issue, or has one of them taken to hide so thicketly that purpose followed thus?"

The men looked at him with a sever countenance. "We ent give a damn about somet hidin thickets. We look fer a girl who we ad saw enter these woods. She as a medium height with brown hair and raggy common clothing. Has ya seen her?"

Daniel shook his head. "Erst your arrival, I scarce saw any a-one more than six inches of the ground, oft so speedily sent that I could not say. But my good sense tells me, all, and of them, were woodland creatures; lest it be the girl hast feet as light as pads and the speed of Atalanta -though you look not as suitors."

One of the men scowled at him. "Quit yer fancy talk. We mean business, or we'll give you a suit; in chains and terminus, as it's put -for fancy- in the gallows."

"None have I seen, than."

"If ya does, find es an tell es, or we'll be comin to see yee agen. Ya be sur of't."

"As thou wish..."

The hired men walked away.

"....I rebuke."

The two emissaries walked on into the forest. "What a prat," said the taller one, who was named Bernard. "His bow hung as e ornament. His sheath put all wrong fer fixing an arrow and es hand hung like a limp fish to it. Eey couldn't use that weapon to save is life."

"How should a bow be ung?" asked the other who went by the name of Jasper.

"Like so," Bernard said, tipping his sword back at an angle.

"I've seen em worn many a way," said Jasper.

"As there's many a snot nosed prat aboot. Just watch how I do, if ya wants to know."

A little while later, in another part of the forest, Emily was walking. She glanced around her with uncertainty, then spoke: "Hours passed and I beget no gain on perfect loss; only perfect loss that yet, seems more pronounced with every step. Neither south, east, nor west prompt me to action any longer as I've tried them all, and all lead to more of the same: tree to brook - brook to tree. Fortunately, my feet do not complain, for they are accustomed to standing; though they had seen as many a mile as mine eyes have, with more the strain." Emily straightened her hair pin, as Suddenly a voice spoke, startling her, but she had enough wits to pay heed to it.

"Bend thy leg girl, or thy foot and mouth will find a complaint." Emily pushed off with her other leg just avoiding a misstep into a rabbit hole.

"Holey! What orator, in heath or bower of this banishing place?" She crouched at a tree, alarmed.

"One who knows a hole from a hairpin."

"As do I," said Emily haughtily.

"Than you are neat, and not a rabbit."

"But who are you?"

"More o' the air, twixt here and there."

"Is that a who?"

"How came *you* here?"

"By and by."

"How lost thou art."

"To none of your concern, I am. Why shouldst thou start with a proper introduction with such enquiries at hand?"

"Please; bid me times good graces, for there is some matter in the spirit of't. I dwell in the trees and among the woodland animals. I am Daniel."

"Well. A start; Daniel. Though you vex me on this account, I Should not seem ungrateful. Strange as it be to hear a voice disembodied, 'twas spoken at the right time for me and might have saved me a twisted foot or more, so I must thank thee, but as a whole, my gratefulness has a tainting of this vexation and my foot has a numbness to its good fortune. As I say -taken as a hole- my foot might sooner be in it than out of it and married to you in debt."

"'Twas a simple ceremony."

"For a fairie or whatever you may be, you have a foolery about you that sticks in the wrong place." Emily began walking towards a large rotted out tree that lay on the ground.

"What place?"

She approached it slowly and walked around its perimeter towards an opening at the other end. "Here, more than there; the throat, more than the air; hollowed, more than hallowed..." Emily scooped up a handful of acorns that were laying on the ground, then continued walking around the fallen tree. "Mislead, more than liege; this, more than that." She looked into the opening of the hollow tree and threw an acorn as hard as she could, then another. "Scoundrel and scoundrel again."

"Ouww. Ho. Oww there." The young man crouched inside the tree crawled to get out while Emily pelted him with acorns. Finally emerging from the tree, he rubbed his sore spots. "They sharp hit there mark!"

"Not as sharp as I would have it, but I can give it another try." Emily threw one more at him as he fended it off with his arm.

"Damn! And welted. What rancor. And after saving your foot."

"Conjecture. And if you did save my foot, it was as a fraud. Dost thou take thyself clever to harass a lost girl who hath wandered hours endlessly in the forest?"

"Thine lostness was my fuller intent to aide and assist to. Thy foot just came about as such whilst I was resting, so I spoke."

"Then you hid."

"That I did. Only for a little whim."

"Did you think I fool enough to believe a fairie spoke?"

"I never claimed as such."

"Oh, thou crafty. That thy words didn't play full on its allusion, they inferred and ascribed by such a pretense, and put it to me that I should make a fool of mineself in believing of its product. And how didst thou concoct such a name for't?"

"From birth 'twas given, and has been mine ever since; so it was easy come by."

"Well, keep it for thine self. Seeing as you choose to shake it at me in the guise of a spirit, expect not to have it shaken on in the form of a hand."

Daniel looked at her apologetically. "Please; why so replete we be of recent incidents? Call them foolish games for a serious distraction that weighs so heavily on thee."

"And who are you than, Daniel?"

"Marlett to the full. Son of Desmond, a trader. I live in these woods and am off to see my friend Lady Abigail. And thine self?"

"Emily."

"Thou art brief in lineage."

"Brief as my name."

"Who be your father and mother. Know you not?"

"I know my name is Emily. And the rest, I care not to speak of right now."

"I am not one to push."

"Then pull.- that outward glance of thine, from its heat and into words that I may know of its concern."

"Persuants, if you must know. We did not entirely meet up by chance. I had sought out to find you after two emissary men had questioned me. They were looking for a girl who's descript is as to you, which may or may not be you in consideration of the other possible brown haired girls about the woods. I did not care for their jib or presentation and so, set out to spare you its effect."

Emily looked down and thought she might not be so harsh to Him. "For that, I do thank thee heartily. But how did you find me?"

"This is as my home. Do you think I would not hear every snapped branch, be aware, every bent twig? You did well to go south-east for they went south-west."

"Good. I hope they keep to it. But should we not go forth?"

"So we will; but if thou seest these two men about with swords at their hip and scowling disposition; ask no questions, hesitate not, but go before me as quick and light as thy feet can carry or hidest thou as still and soundless as mine example; whichever comes first from me. I have my bow and arrows," Daniel patted his sheath of arrows and bow at his side. "But they are ought, of necessity, ere they would disturb the tranquility of our forest home -outside of practice and sport, where they play to a more pleasing and light-hearted game of accounts."

"Will do and agreed."

"Good than." Daniel smiled to Emily and she looked at him with a more agreeable composure.

"Well. Daniel; son of Desmond, the trader. If thoust know the way. Let us be upon it."

"Come."

Daniel and Emily started walking in the direction of Lady Abigail's House.

CHAPTER 3

Lady Abigail threaded the knitting needle through the fabric, pulled out the slack of thread and deftly brought the needle back down, passing it through to her thumb and finger poised beneath the material then prepared to repeat the procedure a little to the left. Her eyes were not entirely on the work at hand though. She was looking out the window at a man who was walking across the field. She couldn't see his face yet and... "Ouch," she exclaimed under her breath, having pricked her finger. It was a quick, sharp pain. She hadn't bothered with a thimble lately and was getting used to stitching without. She instantly brought her finger to her mouth and sucked at the welling spot of blood, pressing her tongue against it. She pulled the work aside to an end table with her other hand and watched the man approach. As he came closer the recognition registered on her face and she awaited a knock at the door. She took her finger from her mouth and looked at the small dot that now reconstituted at the tip of her finger with less prominence. She dabbed her tongue against it then dropped her hand with thumb pressed to finger-tip, as she heard footsteps come up the front steps.

The knock came. Loud, soft, softer.

Abigail got up and walked over to the door calmly and opened it. A man with fair features and a light growth of facial hair stood on the porch.

"Miss Abigail," he said, as if a preliminary to his words which didn't come or took too long.

"Mr. Lewis, you must speak your mind. You have to express yourself or you'll be taken for someone with nothing to say and then people will cease to expect. That's when things get blasè. You wait and see."

"Blasè?" he repeated.

Abigail continued. "Boring, innocuous, staid; lacking of any hearty returns to less than exemplary efforts."

Mr. Lewis looked at his feet then back up at Abigail. "I'm wanting of more to say. I look to it; but I never learnt more than a hammer does in a kettle of fish about proper vocabulary. I was more worked than schooled."

"Than, is a book a plankton? Is a pen a worm? What do you think? They are more easily gotten to than that. If you want of words, find of them. They are available Mr. Lewis."

"Please, Lady Abigail, if you would. Most call me Lewis."

"But is it not your sir name?"

"'Tis as good first, as second."

"Very well" She paused then swung the door wider open.

"Come in than Lewis"
Lewis stepped inside and sang quietly:

Over, over, over the hill,
full, to three quarter, half and then nill,
over, over, over the hill,
first he stumbled and then he spilled.

    "I hope that a tune to your liking isn't a taste to your liking," said Abigail as she led him to the solarium.
    "No miss. Don't touch the stuff anymore." He looked at the paintings that hung on the wall and imagined how the figures in them felt. The man in a floating boat or the one with hat pulled down, laying in the grass.
    Abigail opened the door to the solarium. "Aaaahhh," she exclaimed, taking in the lush surroundings. "Do you see?" She pointed to the domed glass roof. "The sun with a glassy countenance sends a monocular feast of dewy warmth. How the plants revel in it, but some have tethered there secret heart, or had it tethered, and beg for alms I know not of. The sun and life-water being insufficient. Strange, but true."
    Lewis looked. "Seen it and seen it again, I have, and as likened to a blind man, stumbled on methods that baffle me as much as they would a cock or crow, but are deemed good and right by these eukaryotes and treow for whatever reason. It is much a taste for things o' there nature I think." Lewis stepped forward and wandered among the plants. "Maybe a clipping at fore and aft season," touching the leaves of one, "or the meagerest provisions of water for a month, or a lifetime, for they sip instead of sup. More the shade for this columbine; i' the light for these Lilies, where they might stretch well beyond their season with windows surrounding and the elements near nary. There, I promise you miss; Though I learned as a blind man -so to speak- I learned well The secretive ceremonies and desires of each, save the most exotic of them, and those I would eager study if wouldst be, by the granting of this post."
    "Than to it, Mr... unh -Lewis. For what you lack in words at the doorstep, you gather in bushels at the root. And now you yourself can make some, if you do well, as grounds keeper."

Abigail left the solarium and Lewis walked among the plants and inspected there health and lineage and got to know them as it were. Abigail walked back to the parlor room. She went over to the window, looked outside and spoke:

"I worry for you my friend. Of late, your look says there while your hand says here, and somewhere betwixt them I sense an instigator who had caught your eye but missed your hand. Your thoughts hold me at a distance though I am your closest confidante, who knows you well. Who else am I in this? An observer, looking for the signs of your 'secret ceremony'. Some method that I might stumble onto. With this invite, I will see if it is there, And if I may, watch your eye and hand for where they meet to confer." Abigail turned and went upstairs to her bedroom to pick out a dress for dinner later on at her friend Lidia's house. It was a little while later that she heard a knock at the door once again. She came downstairs and leaned in to the door.

"Who is it?"

"A wanderer, who hopes a knock isn't a nuisance. 'Tis I, Daniel."

Abigail swung the door open. "Daniel. You are always welcome." She hugged him, then looked at Emily.

"And who be this?"

"I am Emily," she answered. "We met erst while in the forest." She smiled to Abigail.

"Welcome Emily." She opened the door for them and they stepped inside.

Daniel halted at the front door. "Lady Abigail. Before our feet; these words."

They both stopped and looked him. "Yes Daniel."

"I must give you awares to our circumstance and its entailments, that you be not caught up unbeknownst and find me less than forthcoming."

"Do you think I not see the affliction in her look, in your bearing, of worry and purpose? Is it not too pronounced to unfold at the quick? Come in first; be not too protective, that I be not too sheltered for my own good."

"Forgive me. I forget to look outside my own concerns to the ways of the heart."

"We may by care, be much discerning for others, dear Daniel, but we needs compare notes and find our footing on common ground; so please, come you both in."

Daniel and Emily entered Abigail's house and they went into her sitting room. Emily heard a fluttering sound as they came in and looked to the window where a pigeon sat and flapped its wings. "Ah. A pigeon has taken your sitting room for a roost."

Abigail laughed. "Only that I have coaxed it thus. You see; 'tis not an ordinary pigeon." She walked over to it and picked it up on her hand and petted it. "It is trained. If you'd like, I can tell you the story of it and perhaps it will take your mind off your troubles."

"Please do," said Emily.

"Have than, a seat," said Abigail who sat on the arm chair and gave the bird one more pet, then with a click of her tongue it flew back to its window perch. "Now; Daniel already knows this, so he will have to hear its retelling -lest..." Abigail had a thought. "Daniel. Just a short time before your arrival, I had interviewed and taken under hire a new grounds-keeper, who is currently applying his craft in the solarium. You two could talk up a green hour, I'm sure. As it goes, he has a reluctance around words that seem to evade his mind before his tongue can find them; but his botanical mind is profuse and agile. There, he gets his hands dirty, with pluck and trimmings."

"Than I shall go and see him and leave you both to acquaint." Daniel left the room and went to the solarium and Abigail looked at Emily.

"I wanted to find some time for us. For sometimes a pretty maid as yourself can find trouble that is easier spoken amongst women. Art thee in some trouble?"

"Yes," said Emily. "I have offended an earl and now he has sent two men out to obtain me and bring me back."

"What didst thou?"

"I gave him my knee, when he laid on me, his hands."

Lady Abigail looked at her thoughtfully. "He tried to have his way with you?"

Emily nodded. "He did. And from the telling of my headmistress, I was not the first."

"I know well, what benefit of the doubt, those of title are given, so your decision to flee was perhaps the right one. You may hide out here until these men have retreated, then perhaps he will forget the incident soon enough. I have dinner with a friend to attend later, but Daniel can stay with you."

Emily touched her hand and bowed her head down. "Oh dear madam. I am forever in your debt."

"Think not of it. If by the truth of your story, than it is my pleasure."

"Than, glad I am madam."

"Please. Call me Abigail." Emily nodded and smiled. "How think you, of Daniel?" Abigail asked her.

"I like him, though I fear we did not start off on the best of terms. He had taken opportunity for a play of trickery with me and I took offense to it in my testy mood."

"You'll find he is as keen for a good jest as much as he is heedful of a good danger." Abigail smiled and considered. "So. My pigeon. Do you wish to hear of it?"

"Most certainly. I am fascinated."

Abigail collected her thoughts. "Some time ago a girl had fallen from her horse not far from here and shown up at my door? She was not badly hurt but needed time to rest a sore leg. Her name was Melissa. She told me she was a daughter to a Marquess of the court. I was just beginning to train a few birds to go out and return; that was the extent of their abilities at that time. This girl and I became as friends and when she left, I gave to her, one of them. She was equally fascinated by them and we had decided to try an experiment of sorts. Thus, I told her I had wondered at the possibility of them being true messengers from one place to another rather than simply going out and returning, so we both considered a process we thought might work. She was to take the bird home and let it accustom of its new surroundings, then - go outside, put the bird in a tree where it can see a window -as point- go to the window with some food for it and call it back; repeat it, and then go farther and farther into the woods and let the bird fly back of its own accord. Through this steady process, she was to make her way gradually to here (Its original home) and leave it with me. Whence I did release it, it flew to her window; she then released it again and it flew back here, and from then on it was fixed in memory to its passage and she and I had the swiftest messenger service in all the land. A secret service, if you will."

Emily listened with fascination. "Incredible. But no one took notice?"

"'Tis a bird. Most commonly common. Even if someone saw
her holding it, they would simply think it a trained pet. It is
prepared for its deliveries in private. There is just the one now."

Emily looked at the bird. "Truly amazing. 'Twould beat a horse
by a long shot."

"Yes indeed," said Abigail.

In the solarium, Daniel and Lewis had been discussing the finer
points and theories of horticulture and botanical gardening
indoors.

"I agree; the Juniper is a hardy plant and would do more
adequately in the shallower soil than its predecessor and for eye
pleasing consideration; 'twould appear a good spot," said Daniel as
Lewis made the transplant. Lewis finished putting it in the ground
then rose up.

"I am so glad we had a chance to talk. I don't find lots who care
to go on about the stuff with me."

"Much the same, say I." Daniel looked about. "I think though, I
should return to my friends, now that they have had a chance to
acquaint."

"Yes. And I to my duties," said Lewis. Daniel smiled. "I'm sure
we shall talk again."

As Abigail and Emily were talking, the door opened and Daniel
having returned, walked over to them.

"Ah. Two as such. One: I've known a long while. One: just as
of thus. One brings something new about the other; I see some
smiles come of it."

"You did well to find her Daniel. She has been most pleasant
company which by other turns, I'd have been without.'

"How long hast you known each other?" Emily asked.

"Since I was yea high." Daniel put his hand a couple of feet
above the floor. "She found me wandering as a youngster and gave
to me an errand to do."

"That you be not errant," said Abigail.

"Yes. My word. There's a change of foot -to the letter. From
thus to thus, or here and there, and such, was I interned tacitly to
purpose thereof."

"And oft times a-journed, in service for many round and about the Berkshires."

"As was opportune, but, when not in your employ. Were trees chronicles, whence a youth, I knew well the compendium of the forest, but Abigail taught me to be learned otherwise. 'Twere the measured balances of a guiding hand that ushered me into halls of sciences, philosophies, languages, arts and histories, and revisited there, the matter through conversation. 'Twas she, verily, who taught me to be of mine own deduction, whence again I did emerge from study, with pages a-flutter in the spaces of my mind, to furnish self-thought -influenced thus- as from a fountain of knowledge to an inner trust."

"Whereso books reside," said Abigail raising a hand to her extensive library across the room.

"So, there did I," remembered Daniel. "Where, 'pon a vav, hung my Kappa Alpha Pi, to muse; and make my occupy."

"See how well lettered is he?" said Abigail.

"Oh, yes indeed. A K may be as good as a C too follow a bee, or an Iota might find the way for a missing Jay."

"There is a naturalist alphabet. Such didactic reasoning. Should we go to school?" Abigail asked smiling.

Daniel considered. "A book might suffice."

"Yes! I think I know it. It is very dictionary," Emily said keenly, and they all laughed.

"Hadst thee time for reading?" Daniel asked Emily.

"My learning was on borrowed time."

"Betwixt duties?"

"Nay. In privacy, whence in my chamber for the night, a book from the libraries of my employ, I would devour thence replace of the next morn whilst about my duties in early hour."

"Good girl," said Abigail.

"'Twas good for the girl, me thinks."

Percy flapped his wings at the sill and Abigail looked over then remembered the time. "Alas. As much as I am enjoying this company, I must now make heed to my friend Lidia's house for dinner. I will leave you two to take care here whilst I am gone. My lady assistant Sara is somewhere about, and Lewis, is of course in the solarium."

"Should I accompany you?"

"Daniel, I am fine. It is about an hour on horseback by the strike. You keep Emily company. I'm quite sure Lidia will ask me to stay over. That being, I will leave tomorrow with the sun at a third."

"I will come meet you then on the trail," said Daniel.

"Very well than, Daniel. So, adieu. Feel welcome in my house and enjoy your stay." Abigail smiled to them and left the room then went outside and made her way to the horse stable.

CHAPTER 4

At the same time, Melissa (from Abigail's story) was sitting across a lounge seat in a friend's chamber. Her friend's name was Mariel. She was the daughter of a wealthy ship owner. His estate was in the Anover region and close to the Tayler River where Mariel's father could see and watch over the ships comings and goings. Melissa was watching Mariel's ferret which was running about its enclosure in a corner of the room, while Mariel had left for a moment to get some of her father's chocolate covered cherries, as a treat for them. She returned with the chocolates and looked to her ferret when She heard it rustling about. "Psssst.Quiet." The long skinny creature looked at her and calmed down.

"These are French chocolate cherries. My father just got them from a shipment yesterday."

Melissa picked one up.

"Go ahead," said Mariel, and Melissa and Mariel both tried a chocolate cherry.

"My gosh," Melissa emoted, her mouth still finishing the treat.

Mariel smiled knowingly. "Aren't they wonderful?"

"Mmmh hmmm." Melissa finished her chocolate and looked at her friend.

Just then Mariel's father knocked and opened the door. He had two young men with him. "Mariel. Your uncle Lawrence has just arrived for a visit and with him, he brought your cousin and his. I am going to go riding with my brother. Would you four keep company with each other?"

Mariel looked at her cousin who nodded a greeting to her. "Certainly Papa."

"Maybe you should all go to the sitting room," Mariel's father said (not feeling it proper to have two boys in her chamber).

"Yes Papa. Come Melissa." Mariel and Melissa got up. The two young woman exited to the hall and Melissa looked at their new companions. Mariel's cousin was quite handsome with light wavy hair and an amiable appearance. His friend had a reserved, but sensual expression, dark hair and an observant look. They all went down the hall to the sitting room.

"I'm off, and perhaps to catch a fox," said Mariel's father.

"You get him; soundly, papa," she said, and her father went downstairs. They all went into the sitting room and Mariel slid down onto a high back seat, and Melissa, to one next to her. Mariel's cousin looked at her and smiled, a bit precociously.

"Cous."

"Cous what?" she said, then looked at his friend. "And who's this other?"

Mariel's cousin put his arm on the young man's shoulder. "Harris Donnely. As I cousin to thee, he to me, where the blood is split between us. For you: a father's brother marries, and so you have an aunty; and he stands just that side of her as her sister's second born."

"Auntie's dark hair goes beyond her, yet there its familiar appearance is of a stranger."

"Not for so long," said Harris.

"Good to meet thee Harris, and this is my friend Melissa." Melissa nodded, "Hello Harris."

"And Melissa, you know my cousin Darbey, who owes me a kiss."

Darbey laughed and went over then kissed Mariel quite sensually on the cheek.

Mariel smacked him on his ass. "Fresh. Too fresh for a cheek."

"Soft. Too soft for a spanking," Darbey replied, crouching beside her awaiting more.

"That is all there is for the ass."

"What; does cous call me an ass?"

"You have an ass. Whether you be an ass is another matter; but I will be so kind as to say, you are not too much usually inclined." She looked at Melissa. "I hesitate to guess I may have shocked my friend. Insinuation is a game that can easily become too suggestive," she said glancing at Darbey. "Even for me."

"I am not so shocked," said Melissa, "lest clothes start coming off."

Mariel gasped. "Now it is Melissa who does the shocking."

"Do your clothes not come off so well?" asked Darbey."

"Oh, quite well," said Melissa. "In private."

"Oh. I see. 'Tis a private matter."

"Well, it certainly is not a public one."

"Might you not share your privacy with another?"

"Quite. And there, is the heart of the private matter."

"Does Darbey wish to have a share? Perchance; to deprive her of her clothes, so you might know of her privates?" asked Mariel.

"I dare not say."

"Than, say I. For the proverbial point is made more stiffly then words."

"Is't so obvious?"

"Inch by inch; 'tis so." (Aside to Melissa) "Where-O, where-O, does the hobby horse go?"

"Now, you have my heart in my throat, I should say."

"Pray you then; courage."

"But I will swallow it to its proper place, where in more proper ways of the course, in fondnesses, it may grow -lest by cock, the heart may follow."

"Oh. A fine bed you make. For a wanton and a strumpet. One -the half- is missing. But, that you should find a girl who desires a following heart, I wish you luck."

"And I," said Melissa.

"Then, I will suffice with one who blushes."

"And what of this Harris whose complexion is so flush-colored with lack of words." Mariel observed.

"Miss Mariel. 'Tis but the complexion of the moment."

"Maybe so. But give of us some concession. (Aside to Melissa) *Miss*- Mariel. There is a forfeit address."

"I concede that I am not so unlike my friend. For there is

common heat in my blood that would find no distaste in a willing fling; but, mine heart would not loww me to go where its own doting might not be pinned."

"And so you have seen us as we are. The heart of the matter and the matter of the heart, and never the twain shall part, long as we walk and talk.- and fart," said Darbey.

"Don't!" said Mariel, "or we will leave you to it."

"'Tis only natural; but I shant. I haven't the stomach for it."

"Might we, a word?" suggested Melissa, leaning into Mariel. "We will return presently," said Mariel and she and Melissa got up.

The two young men bowed lightly. "We await your return than," said Darbey.

They went to the adjoining room where they communed quietly. "Wouldst thou act of the things you would speak?" asked Melissa of her friend.

Mariel paused in thought. "With Darbey, as a cousin; a touch or a taste. But me think's, with Harris, I might do as likened, say." Melissa gasped.

"And thee?" asked Mariel.

"Of Harris, my thoughts do not imbue; though Darbey might in private, steal a kiss or two. But if he should try, than softly I'll chide, no buttons or strings, undo."

CHAPTER 5

Abigail rode northward on her light brown mare towards the Berkshire strike, then took it east. She thought about the girl (Emily) quite a lot as she rode. When she reached Lidia's estate she found her outside crouching by a pond. She had a stick and was pulling some algae from the water. Abigail rode up and Lidia stood and smiled to her. "Abigail, dear." Abigail dismounted and they hugged each other.

"Oh. 'Tis well and good to see you again," said Abigail.

"And you."

"What dost thou?"

"Pulling algae from the pond. A questionable act of decorum."

"Why questionable?"

"For the selfish side of regard: to the *unsightly* significance of its *putrid* properties. Foul; but to the fish."

Abigail looked at the large fish swimming about with watchful eyes. "I think they'll get on fine. Could be but the fat of the meat for what we know of their meals. And how is Ferdinan?"

"He is well. Well enough without vouchsafing to a betterment of that wellness. It is the easy comforts we have that can make one prone to shun the downward glance; the studied self-critical eye, for a smile that smiles just to smile."

"Are you not happy together?"

"I have my interests, and he has his, and occasionally we find happiness together, but 'tis too much of the surface; so my happiness retreats back to its moonish integrity to then bare harsh witness, the disappointments of the misbalance to its nature," Lidia sighed. "Whence we retreat to our interests again -and our friends," with a smile to Abigail, "where smiles come easier for me."

Abigail touched her shoulder.

"Come," said Lidia. "My eyes sinks at my critique. There is more to the man than I give credit for. 'Tis my frustrations that speak. He is a good and faithful husband and I, a wife of restless thought and surreptitious desires."

Abigail took her arm and they held hands.

"Let us go in and see my husband and I can show you about the house. It has been awhile." Abigail and Lidia went into the house.

In the dining room of Lidia and Ferdinan Berisfurd, a table was being prepared by two servants, Montegue and Nemo.

Montegue placed the bread plate at a straight angle between 10 and 11, the napkin glass between 1 and 2 by the hands of a clock, the dinner plate serving as such, with points imagined. "Nemo", he suddenly said. "Forks don't spoon do they?"

Nemo thought. "They could attempt it, witheringly I'd imagine, though a spoon trying to fork I'd consider a dismal failure. No point."

"Exactly -my point. And you should take it. It is right over here at this setting of mixed placing."

Nemo walked over and picked up the spoon and fork, one in each hand, switching them so they were in there proper position. He then returned to his station a few settings ahead of Montegue, who looked at him with concern.

"What is it Nemo. Are you more for measure thinking what you should be doing; less by turn doing what you would be thinking?"

"I must confess I was more in thought, but not of doing. So the doing was less the measure of my thoughts than my thoughts the measure of other things; that was so the undoing of that which I should have been thinking and doing."

"Other things?" said Monetgue.

"A remembrance of sorts were in my mind and my eye to the silverware was entranced of it."

"Well, check that one is not encroaching on the others concerns; because if you don't, a guest may tell it for you to all within earshot and the Berisfurds may start to think you forgetful."

As Montegue and Nemo continued their work, Ferdinan Berisfurd (Lidia's husband) entered the room with a small Dachshund trailing behind him.

"My good men Montegue and Nemo. How goes it?"

Montegue responded. "Like clockwork sir, though with a finer design than moving forward."

Ferdinan looked at the place settings. "Yes. Very good."

The dachshund ran to Nemo and played between his legs and he looked down and gave it a pat as the other two considered getting a candelabra. Nemo spoke quietly to it:

"How dost thou feel for a long dog with a short step? Sausagey? I tease, forthsome friend. If you only had words. I can see in your eyes, you ponder them, but haven't the right tongue for it. Probably better without. There - a rub above the ears is as good as a thesis." Nemo rubbed the dog's head fondly then went to join the others as the dog followed about his feet.

Ferdinan watched. "Felix. Leave of poor Nemo. He speaks to you and you pant. You pant to him and he speaks. It's an odd ended bargain, but his fondness of you tempers it. Not the tying up of his feet though."

"Oh. Mind not I sir. He is a true dog to his nature, and of the other thing; 'tis more my doing than his."

"True;" said Ferdinan, "you taunt of nature, as to quell some Pythagorian transmigration. Maybe that is why he likes you. Now to matters at hand. In attendance will be Miss Abigail and two other guests you know not. One is a book seller from Bermont, the other a land commissioner; so you may have a meager tidbit of them afore. In estimate: Say, six o-clock, to eat."

"Good sir," said Montegue.

"Than I'll be gone." Ferdinan walked to the door.

"Know when you're wanted," chided Nemo to the dog and it turned to join its master just as he called it. "Felix!"

When Ferdinan and Felix were gone Montegue turned to Nemo. "Prithee. Now that we have set table, wouldst thou tell me Nemo, of the remembrance you had in your mind?"

Nemo put his hand to his chin in thought. "'Twas of leaving earlier today and of the substantial creaking of the hinges 'pon the front gate, then of a jethro tull and the turning of soil from a plot by a glen, then a bell tower and its ringing, then of a crow that did with importune eye, fix to the west and caw, then of a man through the trees who shot arrows at apples hung by string a-swinging from a poplar tree, who took notice of me and smiled as I passed but said naught, then of a long stretch of tree and brook, brook and tree, then of a hare, then of a peasant girl a-wandering in the wood who bade me if I knew any landowners desiring of assistance or service. I having explained to her that I was not want to keep up on the politic and goings on outside my own place of employ, suggested she try about the court and the northern Regions, to which she sighed easily and smiled not so easily; then of my departure thus filled with back tracking thought of that which I had just seen, and finally my arrival at sir Eglemore's plot to obtain the food supplies and spices after which I travelled the same route back."

Montegue thought. "Hast not thou mixed some chaff with the wheat?"

"Not for the sake of posterity."

"For the trip?"

"Yes. For the trip. I do recognize which characters have import. Be it not the crow and hare, lest our subject be that of hunting for scavenger or sport. Alas; I thought I might give you the benefit of meeting up with them.- by and by, as it were; rather than have them dropped afore you."

"And glad that you have. It was a good trip?"

"Yes. I quite enjoyed it."

"And of thine return; didst thou see the girl and the bowman again?"

"Nay. They had moved on."

Montegue mused. "I must get about oiling the hinges of that front gate."

CHAPTER 6

The Earl of Bale stood in his sitting room with the two emissary men who had been out looking for Emily. He threw and re-threw a pair of dice on a gaming table staring at them as though their falling on the right number was of import. "You simply lost her after you saw her enter the woods," he said disgustedly.

"Sir. She was a good 50 paces afore us and the tree's er in bloom. When we were in em, we could ardly guess at her going," said Bernard.

"Why not split you up and go alternate directions?"

"We thought it better te ave us both to guard er fer when she be captured."

He looked at them with barely hidden contempt. "Where be you two from?"

"We ere long time sailors ooh as taken to our land feet."

"Hath you experience as soldiers or emissaries?"

"Some. Some enough sir."

"That I should be one to tell you how to do your job. And I am supposed to pay you."

"Just the base; fer information without capture." said the man.

"I think not."

"Ya better," said Bernard with calm warning.

"And what if I don't?" said the earl as he walked to the door and opened it. His man servant stood outside. "Any actions taken against me would be taken up swiftly by the royal guard and you would pay dearly. "Dryden," he called, "would you show these men out?"

The servant stood at the door and the two hired men paused a moment then walked towards the door. "You tek care now." Bernard looked him over with an ominous glare as he walked out. They turned and left out the door and down the hall, then exited the earl's estate.

Outside on the walkway, Bernard scowled, "E'el get what's comin to em; somewhere off the record. Et fer now, as we been robbed, we'll ave to do some robbin fer ourselves."

Jasper nodded, "Aye. I'm in't."

CHAPTER 7

Daniel and Emily were in the sitting room of Abigail's estate. Daniel had tipped a table onto a rug. He found it had a slight wobble and was scraping away with his knife at the unfinished leg bottom to rectify it.

Emily went to sit on an oak seat and watched him. "Daniel."

"Yes," he answered.

"My thanks; for bringing me here."

"I am glad I did."

"What think you of Abigail?"

"I very much like her," said Emily.

"There are not many who would let a common woodsman as myself stay in their home; but she would sooner have someone here when she is away, aside from her servants. Sometimes than, she bids me to stay when she is gone. Her father owns a good portion of land in this forest. I occasionally do work for him as well, through Abigail, but my devotions are to her."

"Where do you live?" asked Emily.

"I have a small dwelling east of here."

"And where be your mother and father?" Emily asked softly.

"As a small child, my mother and father were killed. I was raised in an orphanage as I remember, thence I gave it the slip and returned here to wander about these woods out of some memory it seems - and was thus taken in by Abigail. She has been as a second mother to me ever since."

Emily looked at him, taken aback. "My goodness," she said, then mused "I wish I had someone as such."

"Perhaps you will as yet find your mother or father," said Daniel.

"Alas, I do doubt that."

"You have found friends."

Emily looked to him and he was suddenly struck by her beauty in a particular sort of way.

"Have I?" she said. "Though one were greeted with acorns?"

"Oh. I almost forgot," Daniel said with a smile.

Emily smiled as well. "Than, it is less, a sore spot?"

Daniel looked at her then glanced down. (Aside) "As less is the more beguiled; with looks like that."

Emily looked down with a moment of shyness as well . (Aside) "What is in a look; know there I?"

They were quiet a moment. "What do you do when you are not working?"

"I explore, read, practice with my bow, and I am in an acting troupe some of the year."

Emily was surprised. "Ah. I have never been to the theatre. I should like to see you act sometime."

"Never to the theatre. Than, may misfortune remain unattended, till you see what was amiss; thus it won't be amiss no more, and misfortune -as it shows its face- have no further place. You might put it on your list."

"It is."

"Whence the curtain parts, art will find life a new kind of window for your senses."

"Save me a seat."

"Most sightly and neat."

"Can I stretch out my feet?"

"As easy as you please."

Emily smiled. "And there 'Pon the stage, sweet Daniel will be."

Daniel looked at her for a moment, as though noticing something about her for the first time, and (quite out of character) was at a loss for words.

"Might we go see the halls?" asked Emily.

"Very well."

Emily and Daniel went out into the halls of Abigail's estate. "These are the halls," said Daniel.

"That we walk in good conduct," said Emily playfully. "Look there," she enthused suddenly taking Daniel's hand as she pointed with her other hand to a large tapestry hung in the dining room.

"Yes," said Daniel sighingly.

They looked at it more closely. It was very large and intricately Designed with interwoven patterns of flowers, shapes, symbols and combinations of color. As they stood there, Emily moved her fingers slowly through Daniel's fingers.

"Daniel. How your thoughts?"

"They are of most sudden change."

"How so?"

"From easy to enraptured."

"Is it our words that beat about the heart?" asked Emily.

"As much as the red of your cheek."

"I blush to consider."

"And the look of your eyes."

Emily turned and looked at him. "What of my lips?"

"Your lips?" And he leaned in and kissed her softly.- then again.

CHAPTER 8

Lidia had shown Abigail about the house then they went to the sitting room to have some tea and await the other guests. "Might it be, that I know some of your other dinner guests?" asked Abigail.

"I would guess not. I scarcely know them. One is a book seller from Bermont, and the other a land commissioner."

"I do get to the book shops, but I don't frequent Bermont too oft," said Abigail.

"Nor do I. Honestly; I don't know where my husband meets some of these people. We are different in that way. He will invite anyone to dinner that he finds the briefest of satisfactory acquaintance with, whereas I prefer familiar friends or relatives."

"It might make for interesting topic," said Abigail.

"Let's hope," said Lidia. "I can talk of weeding out ponds."

"And I, my horse's diet." They both laughed.

"And our guests will know of the latest books and land holdings," said Lidia. "That makes for a patchwork of conversation."

"Patchwork..." mused Abigail, remembering something as she touched her pricked finger (now a faded red dot.) "Lidia. Your thoughts and desires you spoke of earlier. Might you tell?"

Lidia was quiet a moment. "I do want to. I think that I should."

"Than do," said Abigail touching her arm. "I am your friend. What should you have need to keep from me?"

"You might not imagine what."

"I care not for imaginings, but the truth of it."

"Very well. I have thus been unfaithful to my husband, thrice times."

Abigail looked at her with concern. "Of recent?"

"Yes. He is a nobleman named Andrew Dunlop. I met him just outside the court, at an art viewing," Lidia said, and with a look that came suddenly, she began to cry. Abigail held her and when she had finished crying, Lidia looked up at her and wiped the wetness from her eyes. "Let's not speak of it anymore."

Abigail nodded. "Would you like to see one of our new paintings?" asked Lidia.

"Certainly," said Abigail, and she followed Lidia into a small adjacent room where three paintings hung. Lidia pointed to one of them. It was a portrait of a lady at a well. She held a kerchief in one hand. Her other hand was reaching down as though to grab something. The girl's eyes though turned far to the left as though watching someone or something with a concerned look. There was a coach to her left and a wisp of smoke could be seen rising above the tree line. They both looked at it silently. Abigail was unsure what to make of it besides it being finely done in style and execution. "It is evocative. Who is the artist?"

"His name is Francis Riley." Lidia looked down, feeling better, but spent, from her confession and then they went back to the sitting room.

CHAPTER 9

Francis Riley was at that time employed in the service of doing a restoration of an etching on a stone column within the center portion of the palace gardens in the Royal Court. He was working intently at his task when he heard laughter and a moment later, a young woman with light brown hair dashed by, followed a few moments later by another young woman with dark hair. As he worked he occasionally caught glimpses of the two running about the garden paths and heard their excited starts and giggles. Soon, the first who had ran by came into view again around some rose bushes and dashed up to him half delirious.

"Look sir. Mark her; she's impetuous," the girl got out through starts, and glances, then she dashed behind a bench.

The dark haired young woman soon followed. "Give it up I say, or thus when I catch thee, and soon it shall be, I will strip you of all garment of thine fashion."

The pursued young woman half laughed and sighed then walked about the bench with the other girl following. "Dost thou hear what goes on in the head of a proper-seeming lady of the palace?" she said looking to Francis.

"Francis hesitated a second to reply, when the dark haired young woman lunged over the bench and took the other down by the feet to the grass where she was consumed with gasps of laughter and distress as her assailant got on top of her. Though she struggled, the dark haired young woman was utterly determined to have her way now that they were in such a position.

"The buttons undo…" she lilted and went to her purpose with

quick fingers before coming back to secure the girls flailing arms. "…two by two."

"On my honor!" the young woman on the ground gasped.

"On your honor, what?"

"On my honor, I am sorry I called you the queen's... what I might not mention here," she said, stopping herself short.

The dark haired young woman looked over her for a moment, then darted a glance at Francis. They both calmed and took in some air then the other still pinned to the ground smiled. Her assailant bent down and kissed her on the lips then the tip of her nose, after which, she got up and walked away. The young woman lay on the ground for some moments more taking in air.

"She did not eat you." said Francis.

"No. She did not," repeated the girl dryly, then she buttoned up her dress and got up. She looked at Francis, curious. "What dost thou?"

"A fix for what hath weathered."

"Art thou but a fixer?"

"Nay. 'Tis compensatory to other artful pursuits."

"Which?"

"Which - do I? Portraiture."

The light haired young woman brushed off her clothes and looked at her friend walking across the palace lawn. She mused aloud as though to herself, "She's headstrong as a bull, for such a sprightly thing. I fear it may find her trouble." She was thoughtful for a moment before turning back to Francis. "I know of someone who is seeking a portraiture to be done; if you are good. She will not have a shoddy impression."

Francis looked to the dark haired friend crossing the lawn. "Not..?"

"Goodness no," said the young woman, "Now that would be a job. I should not give her name. Are you than?"

Francis looked to her. "Am I..?"

"Talented?"

"I do my work as best I can. I am not one to say."

She thought for a moment. "Come of a fort-day, at 10 to the half. We have plans for studies. Samples are a must, you understand."

"10 to the half…'twould be…."

"About a rising third quarter, or so."

"Therewith, I can and will bring samples."

"Good than. My name is Lady Michelle."

"A pleasure," said Francis, bowing his head lightly to her."

"Continue about your work. Upon confirmation with my charge, a servant will presently be out with formal invite."

"Well and good," said Francis.

CHAPTER 10

Outside, by the front of the Berisfurd estate, Ferdinan was waiting for his guests to arrive. The first to do so was Peter Arper who rode up in a coach. He got out and they greeted each other warmly. Several minutes later, Maurice Lawton arrived. He greeted him as well and they all stood talking for a while. It was during their conversation that Peter had offered to Maurice, that 'The soil erosion in much of the southern Regions was due,' he felt, 'in large part to water being diverted to the north,' and that, 'a simple triage system of distribution could remedy this.' Maurice replied that 'Land issues were best left to the council, who knew the wider issues and implications.'

Ferdinan brought them in and they walked over to the sofa where the two women sat.

"May I introduce you to my wife Lidia," said Ferdinan. (And to Lidia) "This is Peter Arper; a book seller from Bermont."

Peter gave a pleasant bow. "'Tis a great pleasure madame." He had a paleness of appearance and one shock of his fine hair, longer than the rest of it fell across his face, which he swept back with his hand as he raised his head from his bow.

"Very good to make your acquaintance Peter."

"And this is my wife's friend, Abigail."

Peter bowed again and repeated the process with his hair. "My hair is unruly with bows," he said not too loudly.

Abigail laughed.

"And this," said Ferdinan, "is Maurice Lawton. A land commissioner of the council."

He bowed slightly to both women in succession. Madame Berrisford. Madame..." he looked up at her.

"Bellevue," Abigail finished for him.

"Have a seat friends," said Ferdinan, and he showed them the options of sofa and chairs.

"Ferdinan. Might I use your water room first? My ride was quite long." Asked Maurice.

"Most certainly," Ferdinan said, and pointed. "At the halls end."

"Very good," said Maurice, and he went there.

Peter seemed to hesitate as though deciding whether to await the finish of their exchange or go and sit. Being a brief exchange, he didn't wait long. He then sat a foot or so from the very right side of the sofa. He had a plain wrapped brown package with him that he still had not made mention of, which he placed in the space between him and the sofa arm. Abigail could sense everyone wondering what it was, and thought it might be a good time to get it out of the way because they would soon be eating. If it were a gift, it might rather not be left as a lingering side-script to peoples appetites. If it was not, than let someone put it aside for him.

"Mr. Arper. You have a package?"

He turned to it. "Oh yes. My conspicuous hold," he said, with awareness of its puissance to her mention. She had the thought that perhaps Mr. Arper was not used to formal get-togethers and unsure of when to bring the package up in lieu of other conversation (and with a smile to Abigail) was glad for the bit of assistance in that regard. He had a friendly disposition, though as much, a solitary look about him.

"This is for you Ferdinan. In my perusal of new arrivals, I thus came upon a personal favorite."

"My," Ferdinan said taking it. "And wrapped even."

"Book wrappings. Oh yes. Even on an hours ride, the page edges can tarnish."

Ferdinan pulled off the brown paper and looked at a large book called *Emerland : A Land Through Time.*. It had a brown leather cover and gold trimmed pages. Instantly he began to skim through it right in front of everyone till finally turning his face up with a look of amazement. "Peter. Thou hast rendered me speechless. Thank you my good friend." Ferdinan went over as Peter stood up and he hugged him with the book still in his hand across Peter's shoulder. He walked back to where he'd been and looked into it once more before speaking again. "You'll have me occupied for future hours, I am certain. This will be as a companion to coffee in the sitting room; an elixir to petty boredom that it may become rapt; a sweet balm to sleeplessness that it forget of itself and be not a beggar to sleep, but go gently into it. My gratitude."

"'Tis my pleasure dear Ferdinan. Books are as friends to me, so in the giving, it is like an introduction of one to another."

"Just now," said Ferdinan, "I have perused how Lady Tamara of Basks would keep night watch and that is why her diaries were so full of aloneness and apparitional thoughts associated with such hours. That was why she was first to see baron enemies crossing the river. When all were thought asleep, she was up to give warning."

Peter nodded. "Such a wide and varied history, old Emerland. The best telling of it is in the ones who know their bounds and borders of experience, and relate it, or else have the studious determination to spend ten years of research and another ten of writing to create a tome as this."

Maurice returned and took a seat

"How long hast you dedicated your interest bookishly?" Asked Lidia

"Long as I can remember," Peter replied. "'Twas my father's shop and was inherited to me. First I climbed the books as small mountains then collapsed with them." The others laughed (Except for Maurice). "Then I listened to my father read and discovered they had better usage; then learnt to look into it, page by page."

"Words, mellifluous, fill pages sweet, with nothing done and nowhere been," said Maurice.

"What nothing and nowhere; of the mind?" Abigail asked.

"Bookishness leads to sluggishness, of court, of council, and of pursuit," said Maurice.

"And how do you conceive that?"

"Books should be tools of education and no more, to be looked at for practical information then put aside. One's nose in a book is buried to the workings of the world, which are not bookish, but straight and to the point."

Abigail huffed. "What is straight and to the point? Are courts straight and to the point when they convict an innocent man because they cannot find a guilty one? When the tenets of faulty laws trump reason. Is council straight and to the point when they tax for their mistakes; and pursuit when it is blind to all other views but one's own benefit?"

"All have different pursuits," said Maurice. "They meet face to face and the truer will see the other for what it is."

"Perhaps an enemy to its stubbornness," Abigail replied.

Ferdinand interjected, "Please, please, dear friends, we are here for dinner; and to enjoy."

"I apologize Ferdinan, to you," said Abigail.

Maurice looked to him. "And I as well."

There was a palpable sense of discomfort. Maurice held a staunch Look. Ferdinan tried to clear the air by bringing up some recent happenings at court that he had found humorous. This alleviated the mood some, though Maurice still considered how he might further redress matters with Peter Arper -as discomfiting as this had become to the others- for he disliked him; his awkward mannerisms and hesitantly obscure way of speaking (though in truth it was peter's pointed assessment of the motives behind water issues that had most off-put him.)

Just then, Nemo entered the room. "Sir, Madame, and guests. Dinner is prepared."

Dinner at the Berisfurd's residence was a more agreeable affair than the sitting room conversation had been, as good food and pleasant conversation had influence over all, though Maurice and Peter spoke little to each other. Lidia talked mostly with Abigail, happy to see her as always, and Ferdinan tried to mediate and make his guests feel comfortable. Peter and Maurice left separately afterwards and Abigail was asked to stay the night.

That night, Daniel and Emily were staying up late in Abigail's sitting room. Lewis and Sara had gone to their quarters and they had time for themselves again. Daniel was watching Emily as she stitched the lining of his leather boot which had torn. She began to sing quietly as she worked:

Meet me in Bambrei,
by the bridge and the bend,
with fennel and paper, with needle and thread

tell me a secret,
the one that you know,
that comes half forgotten, until another be told

with boots made for walking,
wherefore and when,
my eyes will turn downward till I'm with thee again.

And so, the day ended.

CHAPTER 11

Daniel and Emily had left early the next morning for Daniel's residence; upon which, Daniel planned to meet up with Abigail and accompany her home, then return to Emily and make some decisions with her as to her current situation. They went out to the stable and found a stealthy looking horse and Daniel mounted then helped Emily up to ride second. The morning was crisp and bright as they came to the wood and stone dwelling where Daniel lived. He dismounted then helped Emily down.

"'Tis of humble compare to whence we were, being but accommodated for shelter."

"And suits me well to that degree. For the space of our hearts care not of walls."

Daniel took her by the hand and they went inside. "Be familiar here, and have a spot for reflection and ease. I must be to Abigail and accompany her home for she should be at leave soon."

"I will than," said Emily, throwing herself comfortably on a down filled long seat. "I will welcome comfort as a lark welcomes the dawn, for it is sweet to me in remiss of its lacking, and I, to its commission; therewith to ponder the elements of such a wondrous day past. May it quell the longings born of thine absence with this, until your return."

"And goodly, may it come you." Daniel smiled to her. "Stay within and let none know you are here."

Emily nodded then got up and kissed Daniel and he left to meet up with Abigail.

Abigail was standing outside the Berisfurd's residence with Lidia at that time, and readying to leave. "Whence there be need, come and speak with me," she said, and Lidia nodded. Abigail smiled and they hugged each other, then Abigail went over to the stable and to her mare which she mounted; then with a wave she was gone.

Abigail rode the trails west and sometime later near the strike, her mare became a touch skittish which she thought due to the cool morning and a rabbit that had dashed out close to the horse's feet. She gave it a reassuring pat and rode on. Suddenly as she rounded a corner onto the strike, two men were standing there with their hands raised in the air. Abigail's horse drew back on its hind legs frightened and she tried to control it. "Easy girl. Easy." She gently pulled the rains as it came down on its front legs then cantered nervously till finally calming enough that Abigail could speak. She looked at them perturbed. "Couldst thou not hear us approach? Why than? Hast neither of thee any sense as to the temperance of a horse, that you choose stand where it come upon you in an instant?"

One of the men pulled a knife from his vest and held it up and the second grabbed the harness of her horse. "Question not our methods. Their results are proof. Now, come down. All we wants is yer currency and valuables."

"You will not," said Abigail angrily."

The one tried to pull at her leg as she spurred her horse on, then the two men shouted and gave chase as she rode off in the direction of her estate. The mare was beginning to pick up stride when Abigail heard one of the men whistle loudly from behind and suddenly a third man stepped out from the trees just in front of her and swung a sword at the horse. Abigail saw within a single moment, the slash that went across the horse's chest, then felt the tightening sinews of the mare's body with the shot of pain and then its trembling muscles as it began to collapse. She seemed to watch from outside herself as she was thrown through the air, then in an instant, she tucked and rolled then tumbled over with a thump that knocked the air out of her. A second later, the horse came down, the ground reverberated, and a cloud of dust rose above. Abigail turned painfully on the ground and touched the horse's face, holding her hand to it as it struggled for breath.

Daniel, after having left Emily, rode southward at a good steady pace. He took the same paths that Abigail had. He started to grow nervous early on when he came upon more hoof prints that diverged from some secondary trails. The others looked to be following the prints of Abigail's horse. He spurred his horse from a canter to a gallop for a while. When he came near the strike and the tracks looked fresher, he dismounted, tied his horse in the trees and went on foot. It was after walking an uphill that Daniel saw at a distance, Abigail sitting on the grass beside the trail. One man stood next to her with a sword and two others stood at a distance, discussing something. Without hesitation, he went into the trees and stepped quietly under cover closer to where the men were. Daniel watched where their feet were situated. It was the one, closest Abigail that he fixed on. He shouldered his bow then from his quiver at his side, he took an arrow and clinched it. Daniel then emerged back onto the path. He spoke in the instant they saw him and knew how quickly he must act.

"Move away from her, or die."

All within seconds, he could see the flourish of movement

among the men, but it was the one closest Abigail who did not move away but began to raise his sword to her that he focused his bow to. It was the momentum of movement that he practiced with his apples: to hit one between ascent and descent, as it swung to its lowest point pendulum-like from the branch of the tree. He did not choose the object in motion here (the man's hand with sword) but took its motion as his cue and let the arrow fly. With a whistling swiftness it pierced through the front of the man's neck and at the same time as he dropped his sword, a line of blood ran down his neck to his vest and he fell. Daniel snatched and clinched another arrow pointing it at the next man who was about to approach Abigail, then hesitated.

Abigail quickly rose to her feet and walked away from them to where Daniel was. He could see now, how distressed she was. Her dress was torn and dirty and blood was running down her leg. She shook her head. "No more. Shoot no more of them."

"I shant; if they don't invite it." Daniel faced them. "You do not treat a lady in such a base and brutish manner. Even amongst thieves, that is understood."

Bernard looked down to the dead man on the ground. "Was he who scuffed er up."

"Abigail. Are you much hurt?" Daniel asked. "Not so much as 'twould appear."

"If you can, you must go now. I will catch up with you, soon enough. Are you well enough to ride?"

"I believe so."

Daniel went with Abigail to the assailant's horse which stood at the side of the trail. He knelt beside Abigail, keeping his bow aimed at the two men. "Step 'pon my shoulder to mount, if you may." She did and mounted the horse using her good arm to support herself. "Be careful. I will await your coming," she said with a concerned look.

Abigail rode off towards her estate and Daniel watched the two men silently till it grew quiet.

"We are meeting too oft for my liking, all of a day."

Bernard looked more closely at him. "Weren't you an actor in that public show at the, ah... round? It were some't about eatin kids."

"I have no desire to discuss it with you."

"What's en actor doin with a bow?"

"Why; pointing it at you." Daniel could tell the taller one who had spoken to him was most dangerous from his casual and taunting manner and his attitude to the situation.

"I am an actor. 'Tis true," Daniel said in an oddly congenial way. "What circumstances befall one so unsuited to the purpose, yet one must suit up to it; as a painter who burns his canvass to lack of warmth; a priest who holds his fist to lack of peace. With sickly pallor of displacement, one must sometimes be as one would not. Will we act than foes? You have brought it to me and left me no exit, but that it would portend your crooked ways in lieu of this. Hence, we will now make leave to the royal guard, or we end this scene.- here; that I may exit from it alone and know it finished for what it is: An act of misfortune. 'Tis your choosing."

The two men watched him with growing agitation and Bernard began to step restlessly back and forth.

"With this step, this indecision; away, or no?" Daniel mused. He suddenly kicked a clot of dirt up at Daniel and came at him...

The arrow flew and pierced his chest and Daniel snatched and clinched the next arrow from his sheath as Bernard fell to the ground, the arrow deep inside him.

Jasper looked stunned, then stood and grew pale with fright. "Do as thou would," said Daniel.

Jasper fell to his knees and began to cry out "I am but a slave to another's demands... as e work horse, as e ignoramus, as e patsy to his mistakes. Spare my life and I'll give you vengeance where it's good, en worthy Fer us both."

Anger flushed Daniel's face. "I don't want vengeance! I want freedom for those of Berkshire to live as they should choose and not have to worry at fighting for their lives at every turn! Stay away! You hear; stay away!"

"I will," he pleaded. "I've enough of't. I did her no harm. At your mercy, I'm back to sea and won cum ere agen."

Daniel slackened his bow and put the arrow back in its sheath. Jasper fell from his knees to the ground and lay there breathing heavy as Daniel stood in thought then looked to him again. "These men must be buried," he said heavily. "Drag them to your left. There is a ditch beneath some rocks about ten paces in. Place them in it then fill it. Be quick about it."

Jasper looked up then rose to his feet. He walked over and grabbed Bernard's lifeless legs and started dragging his body into the trees.

CHAPTER 12

Abigail rode at a fairly slow pace so as not to jostle her wounded arm. She had lessened her fall somewhat by tucking and tumbling when she hit the ground as her father had taught her to do when she was a girl. Her arm took the brunt of the fall. The bleeding on her leg and her dirty dress came from small rocks on the ground where she had tumbled, and being rough handled by the first assailant. As she approached the estate she saw Sara run out onto the lawn, and then Lewis followed.

"Oh dear," Sara said in shock.

"Would, that you can help me from this horse. My arm has taken injure," said Abigail.

Lewis looked about. "One moment," he said.

He ran beside the stable and picked up a cut section of a tree trunk and hauled it over. Lewis stepped onto it then put one foot on a stirrup to reach Abigail. Sara held the horse steady and he lifted her down to where Sara took Abigail's good arm and supported her as she stepped to the ground. Abigail put her arm over her shoulder. "Are you able to walk?" Sara asked.

"Yes. The worst of it did spare my legs." She walked to the house with a slight limp. As they entered the front doors, Sara said to Lewis, "I will bring her to the guest chamber. It is closest. Get a basin and wash cloths. They are by the wash cupboard."

Lewis went and did so, and Sara brought Abigail to the bed and set her down on it.

Abigail sat up and supported herself with her good arm.

"Do you not wish to lay down madam?" asked Sara.

"No. I am alright as such."

Sara began to reach for the buttons of her dress. "May I?" Abigail nodded and smiled to her.

Lewis brought the basin and wash cloths then went to the door. "I will await outside the door." He began to leave.

"Lewis," called Abigail. He turned back to her. "Go to the front entrance and look out for Daniel. If he is not here within five and twenty, do go and seek him out along the trail."

"Yes Madame." Lewis exited the room.

Jasper had dragged the bodies into the woods and deposited them in the ditch, filled it and was now back to the trail where Daniel awaited him.

"Thou must do as you have yourself promised. To the ports, and tarry not a whit. You have no more business here. Dost you agree, or would you harbor deceptions which are the most natural parcel of the trade you took?"

"'Tis no more my trade, but my regret to carry," said Jasper. Daniel looked at him observedly.

"Why were you in attempt to rob this most honorable lady? Was not your employer's pay adequate for you?"

"He paid us not, but withdrew of his promise," said Jasper. Daniel thought. "What is thine employer's name?"

"The Earl of Bale."

Daniel studied him a moment longer. "Go."

Jasper walked off with a dejected look then raised his head in the direction of the Broadmoor Region and the shipping ports. As Daniel considered something, Lewis approached on horseback. He had waited five and twenty then come to seek him out.

"Well to see thee, Lewis," said Daniel in a subdued voice. "How fairs Abigail?"

"Well as can be expected for such a fall. Her arm is quite bruised and she bears some cuts."

Daniel nodded. "I must retrieve my horse, then we have a job to do." Lewis waited for Daniel. When he returned on horseback, he followed him to where Abigail's dead mare still lay on the trail. Daniel proceeded to tie ropes from the horse he'd rode from Abigail's stable and the one that Lewis came on, to the dead mare, then he and Lewis had the horses drag its body into another wooded area (a task which the animals were visibly troubled by) where it was covered with brush. They then took to the trail and made their way back to Abigail's home.

Upon Abigail's departure that morning, Lidia had went to sit in the parlor feeling a restless change of temperament that came with an excited flush to her cheeks. She went over to the sun-dial several times to check it and looked from the sitting room window anxiously. A short while later she went for a walk in the woods. It was some time later, after walking past the birch and ash, hawthorn, and cherry trees that she sat down by a glade. Within a few moments she heard the sound of footsteps and turned to see her lover Andrew approaching. Lidia got up and smiled, watching him, then he spoke.

"My little fetch. How besottedly you teach my most lyric thought of you, of beauty, even beyond its musing."

Lidia went to him and he ravaged her clothes and stripped her naked, then arms entangled, they lay in the glade together. After they had exhausted themselves, they both got dressed then Andrew got up to walk about.

Lidia looked to him. "'Twere that I saw a dear friend and told her that we are lovers."

"Than let us be not, in trepid complicity. Break thine chafish tether of matrimony and allow the hearts rite its full-due."

"Lidia sighed and looked down.

"May't be, that I might find the wayful course to. 'Tis harrowing, sickly-sweet - the endeavor; To renounce the heath of the past, for new found pleasure."

"Doth not this hearts content give reason?"

"But for one, who is undeserved to its cost."

"Is his complacency so innocent; so apt in deception that he should not wake to its effects?"

"Were it so, but that he rather should, he might awake, ergo; as a babe in these woods."

"Alack, it has been as a shrill fife to me that such maladies of experience dote on thy thoughts, to off-color the hue of thine complexion."

"'Tis a lusty complexion."

"Is that the sum of't?"

Lidia looked up at him sweetly. "Nay. Smile, to remind me of the fuller hue, for my heart is made well to its betterment by compare. In diligence, it doth wean itself of belabored languid oaths, day by day, moment by moment, with delicious speed to my lovers eye -that we may soon lay, and not lie."

"Than, tend to thy thoughts here, and let them keep good time for thine heart."

"In this sheltering glade?"

"For now. For now, my sweet."

That same morning, the Earl of Bale was thinking about his planned travels to Italy and France which he was leaving on in two days. He was glad he'd been able to evade the costs of the emissaries and to incur additional funds to spend on his trip.

CHAPTER 13

Melissa awoke that morning in a guest bedroom, looking up at a large colored sketching of the continents which was hung on the opposite wall from where she lay in bed. There were small ships on some of the waterways and smaller arrows which she thought must indicate either shipping routes or tide patterns. She traced up the Tayler River on the map with her eyes to where they presently were.

Mariel and she had spent the rest of the previous afternoon with Darbey and Harrison, or more-so; Melissa had spent time with

Darbey, and Mariel, with Harrison. The two boys had left near nightfall when the two fathers had come back. After returning to Mariel's chamber for a glass of wine, Mariel had shown Melissa to the present guest room where she had now awoken. Melissa, after laying there thinking about all this for a moment, began to feel restless and wished to be headed back home - though... perhaps a walk through court rather than take a carriage, to get some air and possibly hear or see some news along the way. With this in mind, she went and got a quill and paper from a small desk in the corner of the room and began to write a note.

Dear Mariel

I woke early, with a moment's confusion; forgetful of not being in my own room. If I stayed any longer I would feel obligated to call it *la vacances* and eat more chocolate cherries. I need to get back now to my responsibilities and familiar ways. I decided to quietly slip out and allow you your sleep. We must do it again though.

Had a delightful time,
Melissa.

Melissa dressed and stepped quietly down the stairs, then went out to the street. She was a few blocks from Windhem Place, which ran the length of the Anover Region to the center of the court in the west. She walked over to the street and took pleasure in the sunny day and watching people stroll about. She could not walk the whole of the way, so she waved a coach down to take her as far as the Royal Court. From there, she would walk home. The coach that Melissa had gotten was the double seated shared kind, which was less expensive. Money wasn't an issue with her. She preferred though, to have some company for the ride.

The coach pulled up and Melissa got in and sat down then adjusted her dress. "Good day," she said to the other passengers in general. Directly across from her sat a middle aged woman with glasses and a curious expression. Her face looked somewhat flushed, as though she had just been in some heated exchange. Next to the woman sat a man with unkempt black hair. His

shoulder leaned against the frame of the cab and he looked at
Melissa with a kind of feverish ascertaining. The third occupant
who sat next to Melissa was a stoic looking gentlemen who was
looking at the black haired man. With a suddenness of voice that
near shocked her the man with the black hair began to speak. He
leaned in to the woman beside him.

"And you madam. Do you believe in ghosts?"

She looked fascinated and somewhat repulsed at the same.

"I believe in that which is given with due evidence to the
senses."

"Than art thou an atheist, or dost you believe in some kinds of
ghosts?"

"There is due evidence there. It is the word."

"I assure thee. I found words. Whence I had been sent
skittering across the floor 'pon a wooden chair by no volition of
my own and looked back at my pale faced companions still at the
table where we had evoked this spirit, I distinctly heard words
spoken erst while the table stamped its legged feet 'pon the floor -
and I say stamped, as that is how it appeared to me: as the
conscious vigorous stamping of an unruly child having a tantrum.
Then as if by the effect of our own processes, the disembodied
voice found a seamless transition unto the throat of Sir Ballantine
who closed his eyes and spoke its strange musings and –dare I say-
threats. 'Twas then his hand as if by another's will, grabbed the
bowie knife from the sheaf of Reginald who was sitting aside him,
at which point all and everyone scattered across the room to
witness Ballantine -or Ballantine's person- carving words into the
table, top to bottom, with the knife."

The man to Melissa's side looked at him with calm distaste.
"Bah. What stories the besotted mind can weave. What tricks it can
play upon itself. Add unto that, the opium den and its distorted
rearrangement of all the senses and one hast quite a stew. Please
don't expect others to partake of it though sir."

The man looked down. "I do freely confess to being an addict.
It is my base quotidian elixir that doth rob me of my own will to
crave of its own. I do know however, what I saw." All were quiet
for a moment then the man shouted, "Driver. Here please."
The coach slowed then came to a stop. He looked at the others and
Melissa with one more fevered glance, then got up. As he did, a

glass vial stained with the sticky black substance fell from his coat pocket to the floor of the coach. He bent and picked it up, then exited to the street.

After he had exited and the coach began to move again, Melissa looked at the lady across from her who met her eyes and half smiled and shook her head.

"I've heard about him and his group," said the man. "They gather in there hovel weekly to obliterate their senses with opium then commune with the spirit world, whence there mind has little tether left to this world and is itself -as some wayward spirit- as easily influenced by what is not there, as by what is."

"Strange," said Melissa "How some seem to always wish for something else than this - some other; other consciousness; other way of being. I understand, wanting to improve oneself and become more fully aware, but to do it at the behest of opium and ghosts. Where is one's own achievement in that?"

"And what are one's ghosts?" said the lady across from her.

"Quite," said the gentlemen. "Even if, in all the opium haze, there were some truth to any of it, it seems a reckless clambering of lost souls to bear witness to."

"Indeed," said Melissa.

The coach drove on and Melissa leaned over to the woman across from her. "May I ask your name madam?"

"'Tis Jane. Jane Harlow. And you?"

"I am Melissa Whitstaff." They shook hands.

"And you sir," asked Jane of the man.

"Alistair Rume," he said and bowed slightly to both women, then looked at Melissa. "Whitstaff - of the Marquess?"

"Yes. The same," said Melissa "I am his daughter."

"Ah; It is not too often that a lady by such title is seen riding the common coaches."

Melissa shrugged, then turned back to Jane. "How hast your trip been?" she asked her.

"Quite well. I am of an errand for my employer. I enjoy carriage rides and outings. They refresh me and show me much of life outside my knowing. And thee. Have you been on a trip as well?"

Melissa nodded. "To see my friend, where we did little and said much. Empty leisure can be a fine vessel for words to fill though, if its emptiness be not vacuous; if its face be not sullenness. We did later have some young men for company. Something of the boyish wanton and the brooding sensualist in them, all eager with finger words or fondling thoughts; but my friend –in the know- trumped and teased in equal turn; thence, we found them alone to have a somewhat sweeter, more balanced complexion."

The woman laughed. "Ah, to try the woos of persuasion." She sighed. "I would much like a good day of empty leisure. My time spent in this carriage might be my most likened to it, though it be deemed work -but pleasures occupy is never so put to terms." Jane said, smiling to Melissa." Melissa returned her smile. "Alas though. Here is my stop. But, a good ride -spirits and all. Driver, here please!" she called. "'Twas well to meet you both," she said with a nod to Melissa and Alistair.

"And you miss," said Melissa, and the woman got up and exited the coach. "A fine madam," said Melissa musingly to her remaining coach mate.

"Very so." Alistair replied.

CHAPTER 14

Sara had finished helping Abigail clean and wash her cuts and had put her arm in a sling, when Abigail decided she wanted to go to the sitting room. They did so, and after a short while, they heard then saw the two horses approaching outside the window and Abigail sighed with relief. After dismounting, Daniel and Lewis went inside and into the sitting room. Daniel went and knelt at Abigail's side. She smiled and touched his head and he looked at her arm.

"Is it broken?"

"'Tis but badly bruised. Sara though, suggested a sling." Daniel looked down.

"Daniel," said Abigail, "now is no time for awaiting privacies. We are amongst friends; so I must ask thee. What became of your encounter with the men?"

He stood and grew contemplative. "The one had murder and mayhem afixed in his eye. Only that he be pardoned from my sight, I knew 'twould be his purpose, so, I assured him that he must be put to terms. He would not have it -and in so, did he fall. The other looked on him as a cypher awaiting a helping of will; at first, struck dumb when he saw the man felled, then gently pulling his own strings away, as from some puppeteer commandant I saw the brunt of his beleaguerdness rail in the ken of his being and I let him go in trust. They were the same of cause to Emily's plight."

Abigail looked down. "I am most glad that you are well."

"And I, you," said Daniel.

They were quiet a moment. "Daniel; could you do something for me?"

"Of course."

"I ask that you go and tell my father of what has happened for I was to visit him tomorrow and no longer can I."

"I will."

PART TWO - COURTIERS AND COMMONERS

CHAPTER 15

Melissa had gotten from the coach upon reaching the court. Her father's estate was west of the main palace grounds. She began walking and saw the different people about, most of whom were royals, nobles and various northerners. As she neared the square Melissa heard a woman's voice call her.

"Melissa!"

She looked to her right and saw her friend Guendoline sitting with her feet in a fountain. She went over to her.

"Guendoline. You linger well."

"It is a well spot to linger."

Melissa leaned in and gave her a hug.

"Come. Put your feet in. It is pleasant," said Guendoline.

"I will then." Melissa stepped up on the ledge and took her shoes off then put her feet in the fountain.

"I am awaiting the professor for lessons at the conservatory, where he is to teach me the flute. I prefer there rather than home till the stops don't stop me in prelude to partita, and the fingers learn to not mis-step the half, whole."

"'Tis to be expected at the outset," said Melissa.

"Maybe expected, but hardly respected. I wish to articulate my progress first, before my progress articulates me."

"Where is your flute?"

"He will have one for me. Look," said Guendoline. "Sir Langton approaches."

"He does."

"Greetings Sir Langton."

Sir Langton came over to them "Dear Lady Guendoline." He bowed and kissed her hand. "And dear Lady Melissa." He kissed her hand as well. "So pretty over here by the fountain. You looked, in the mist, as a couple of nymphs emerging from Alpheus to Arethusa, but now I see you only have your feet wet"

Guendoline sighed "Ah, *rinfrescante*. We have dried in the sun."

"So then, I should be out of breath," said Melissa.

"Oh, come. I've seen you both hold your breath through ceremonies longer than a swim, whilst at the royal courtier's inductions."

"Your eye is just too slow. A careful woman can sneak in a word between the dubbing sword and a lord's lapel," said Guendoline.

"I shall watch more closely next chance I get," Langton winked.

"So what brings thee out today?" Asked Guendoline.

"A play being put on."

"There is a play?" inquired Melissa?

"Yes. A free production of the Wayfarers at the Round." He looked at them with their feet in the water. "This is a fount of reason; but I shall ask. Besides.- another reason you are here?"

"To learn the flute," said Guendoline.

"How pointless. And you Melissa?"

"To hear the flute."

"How delusional."

"Oh fa! The flute is coming. I have paid for it; and my lesson to the professor."

"I think it is dropped by a king, played by pan, left in a tree, found by a fool, stole by a thief, and held for ransom as an image to thee."

"Why?"

"Because. It is not a flute at all. Can you enter the conservatory?"

"Yes."

"Neither can he."

"What mean you, such nonsense? I said yes."

"And so you should have, and said no to what he propositioned, for he knows not how to play the flute. He knows how to make money of nothing, or a nothing-fashioned image."

"Who is he?"

"Now? A man in a cell. I saw him on my way here. He was trying to play himself a ticket to Spain. You were his last lesson. He is quite mad. He was playing no flute up the court house stairs. He did that well justice to his madness, I must say -with stops and all."

"How can someone get away with it?"

"He hasn't. Go to the courthouse and you will get your money back; which I recommend going into the conservatory with, for anyone can sit on the front steps there and claim to be a visiting professor of music."

"Incredible," said Guendoline. "My thanks Sir Langton. Now I will to the courthouse."

"Goodbye fair ladies." Sir Langton turned and went to get a coach and Guendoline and Melissa went to the courthouse.

Upon entering the courthouse, Guendoline could hear the mad professor playing his imaginary flute from the cells.

A guard approached her. "Good day madam."

"The madman took my money for a flute and lesson," said Guendoline.

"I must confirm it with him madam," said the guard.

"Confirm it with *him*?"

"Who else?" asked the guard.

He took them into the cell block and over to the professor's cell where he was still playing.

"Ay," the guard shouted.

The professor stopped and looked up at Guendoline and smiled. "Are you here for your lesson?"

Guendoline looked at the guard with satisfaction.

"Well enough," he said.

As they began to walk away, the professor played a short passage then jumped up and shouted. "Do, re, mi, fa, sol, la, ti, do. Find the root!"

Guendoline had her money returned then she and Melissa left and walked over to the conservatory.

Once there, Guendoline sighed. "I don't much feel like taking a flute lesson anymore. Perhaps later. There is the play that Langton told us of. Would you care to?"

Melissa smiled, half to herself. "Yes. Let's do."

"Come than," said Guendoline and they went to find a coach to the playhouse, which was in Anover where Melissa had just come from.

CHAPTER 16

Daniel left Abigail's estate and rode towards her father's which was in Anover. After some distance, he stopped in a glade by a small lake. He dismounted and went to the water where he kneeled down and washed his face, then as he looked up, he noticed a swan in the distance. It was swimming away from a small island which was situated in the center of the lake. The large swan moved slow and steady towards him as though curious at the new visitor. As it neared, it craned its neck and made a throaty sound. Daniel stared at it, then suddenly his eyes were drawn beyond it to where in the periphery of his vision, he thought he saw movement on the island. At a glance, he thought it to be a dappled bird of some kind rummaging in the thickets. It was a very small island -maybe twenty paces in length- and not very hospitable, as it was covered in overgrown vegetation and jagged stone. After making its ambiguous point and looking at Daniel, the swan turned and began to swim back. Daniel watched the island and the swan for a few moments more. The swan then swam out of view behind the island and Daniel went over to his horse, mounted it and rode on.

It was a while later that he arrived at the residence of Abigail's father, Bertram Bellevue. Daniel approached the door of his estate then knocked. A servant answered. "Sir. You knock?"

"Good day. I have wish to see Mr. Bellevue, if I may."

"And what is it of concern?"

"His daughter, Abigail. I am a friend to her."

"Thine name?"

"Marlett, Daniel. He knows me."

"A moment."

Daniel turned and looked to the west where the more common class shop district of the Anover Region was, and could see the high roof of the Round (The playhouse where he most often had his employ and parts in productions.)

The servant returned. Daniel looked to him. "The master has declined to see you."

"Than simply tell him, his daughter Abigail has taken a fall from a horse. She is not of serious injury, but she will need time to recuperate."

"How was this fall taken?"

"Do you ask of your own behalf or his?"

"His, I do."

"Should he desire further knowing, he should visit his daughter, for as you have informed me, I have no more business here."

Daniel went back to his horse and rode into the shops district of Anover, then towards the playhouse that he had been looking at. He smiled as he neared it, having not been there in a while. He dismounted and tied his horse up to a post, then stopped to look at a leaflet that was posted on the wall of the building.

The Wayfarers
On the 30th day of April
One performance only, Dusk curtain
Free to all. Come early

Daniel walked up to a large set of doors and went inside. As he walked through the front promenade he could hear a voice emoting loudly from the stage. He stepped into the back of the playhouse and watched two men on stage acting out a scene in the empty theatre. The vested man stepped towards the other who was writing with stoic character at a desk.

Guest - Why dost thou pretend to be a man of letters?
Fool - Pretend? I am a man of letters. Here I sit -a man- and here (holding up letter) is a letter.
Guest - Your name is but a frame and you make a false picture to its signature.
Fool - 'Tis a pseudonym.
Guest - You are not he, sirrah.
Fool - I am, who I am.
Guest - Thou perpetrate a falsehood.
Fool - Not I, Not I.
Guest - Yes you, Yes you.

Fool - Than who?

Guest - A fool.

Fool - Where is proof?

Guest - A maidservant told me, she observed you in passing, reading a book upside-down, then to smile upon righting it the next moment as though pleased at thy succession of propriety.

Fool - I had picked up the book from a table and opened it to a story of a man stuck in the belly of a whale. I read of his suffering to this fate for three days and took pity on his plight. I wondered to myself; 'might I help in some way?' A thought then came to me, and in such, I turned the book upside-down just as the maid was passing and greeted her. Whence she had passed and I righted the book again, I smiled to think upon the very next line, as the whale made queasy, vomited the man upon the shore.

Guest - And a fool doubly, who thinks himself God.

Fool - God? I am no God.

Guest - No. A fool. For you cannot make whales queasy by the turning of a book.

Fool - You say it was a God made the whale queasy?

Guest - As is told.

Fool - I didn't catch his name. Which was it?

Guest - The Christian God.

Fool - Doth he and Jove get on well?

Guest - They are of different persuasions.

Fool - Well, I hope they might not meet, for Jove has a testy temper, and might make a scene of it.

Guest - And I too, should you persist.

Fool - I will speak no more of Gods than.

Guest - Rather, speak no more.

Fool - I was not brought up rude. Whence spoken to, I speak in return. Do you like good bread?

Guest - What has that to do with anything?

Fool - There is good bread in the kitchen, so it has to do with your belly and my offering.

Guest - I offer you this. I shall inform your master of whom thou art.

Fool - And he shall inform you of the door.

Guest - I think not.

Fool - Thou dost think to thy benefit, but thy benefit might not think to you.

Guest - There is no benefit in it for me, but to show his fool plays as a nobleman and gives away his bread.

Fool - And I to show his guest has bad humors.

Guest - Hogwash.

Fool - Nay. 'Tis good food.

Guest - Hogwash, I say.

Fool - Properly? Dost thou think me a proper fool? They'd be dirty again before putting the scrub brush away. But, half a laugh may be a snort; so I will round them, roundelay.

Guest - Fie.

Fool - ...dee die diddle, fie dee die dum,
hogs in the middle, the washing be done.
Fie dee die diddle, fie dee die dee,
that feed on such words, 'twould make muddy of me.

Guest – Be-gone you knave; or fetch me a barrister.

Fool - Why a barrister? Does he laugh?

Guest - Because you tax my patience with your ramblings; so I should claim misappropriation in a court of law.

Fool - Than I shall claim malapropism to your misappropriation with due evidence of the distinction between taxes of the state and of the mind. One's words are not responsible to what services another's patience expects; therefore, one's patience might pay (when taxed) faux funds of temperance at its own behest, and cannot hold the instigator accountable to the use of those funds, nor should even presume the instigator a tax collector, per se, in lieu of or in further distinction of the afore-mentioned accused role: as parleyer -wittingly- of ones currency of character -which may be taxed.

Guest - What?

Fool - A fool.

Daniel burst out laughing at the back of the aisle and they both looked to the back of the dark theatre.

"Our solitary audience sounds familiar. Might we put a face to a laugh!" shouted the man playing the guest, whose name was Merchant.

"Give us physic!" said the other, who went by the name of Kip.

Daniel walked down the aisle to the stage.

"Ah. Daniel." said Merchant. The two men hopped down to greet him.

"My good friends. Your scene hath played of felicity to my darkened day."

"Than wean yourself of it. So well to see you. Have you come to see our production?" asked Merchant.

"I have just now read of it 'pon a leaflet; I may, to that."

"Sit you down with us," said Merchant.

"We can much use a leisure break as well," said Kip.

"For certain. We have done much work on the production. Kip and I, among others. Tell me Daniel. Why has it been a darkened day for thou?"

Daniel looked hesitant then downcast, as they both looked to him. "It has been a time of trial for me up to whence I arrived at the Round. My dear friend Abigail, whom I have long been charge and patron to, was assaulted by mercenary thieves in the Berkshires. I having come upon them, took two of their lives."

"For sooth," said Merchant heavily, then paused. "Was she harmed?"

"She took an injured arm, bruises and cuts and has lost her mare in the incident."

"My thoughts be with her," said Kip.

"And mine," added Merchant.

"Thanks friends."

"Did you know much of them?" Merchant asked.

"They were mercenaries hired to return a young woman named Emily. She had employ as maidservant to a certain Earl of Bale. This man had not paid them for their services and hence, they robbed in turn."

"I am at your assistance in this matter, if required," said Merchant. "And I," said Kip.

"My thanks," Daniel said.

Merchant looked at him with concern. "Come Daniel. We are your friends. If you would to; do share your thoughts."

"This Emily; she and I have become close and she has been much of my mind. Upon taking leave this morn, looks and words and hours with her did stay with me. No longer did solitary wandering enthuse me, but as passages between whence I saw her and whence I should see her again. Even with scarce a thought, my breath did come with the blushing of her cheek and go with the turning of her eyes in memory's soft hue. I did wander in reverie like this for long. Thence; to come upon these brute thieves and the sight of Lady Abigail having been assaulted by them. Therein I did feel such a shift and the outcome of violence, then all its afterthought and heaviness. It is in this that I am vexed. My heart issues my mind; my mind checks my heart, and both seem at struggle to make overture, for the displacement I felt of keenness to my forest home did trouble me, and yet I do not want to be a foolish wanderer who walks endlessly and hangs his thoughts in the trees of silent visage; for I think I am in love with her -my dearest Emily."

Kip and Merchant listened attentively, then Merchant spoke. "Such influence of passions doth quell my words."

"How the heart forgets. Cupid's arrow must color me naive," sighed Daniel.

"Hardly; lest naivety is love's common folly."

"I must make a confession. I had come here to find this earl; and for vengeance. All of the day hence though, I have weighed the effects of this and thus; stopped myself, that I should not bring further woe. Alas. I was in such a state, and had need to give voice, I have been away too long and must go to Emily soon but I had much want to pay you visit first."

Merchant was thinking. "Daniel I have an idea. It is fortuitous - as to character. An idea to ease one's troubles and employ one's mind and vigor; for there is a role available due to an inebriated player."

"What say you, Merchant?"

"Upon his way to the theatre today Kip saw one Maimar -who was to play the character of Marco- measuredly intoxicated and stumbling from the door of the Pig and Whistle tavern. If he cannot walk straight, I cannot trust him to talk nor act straight. Kip or another could go and obtain your Emily and inform her of your well-being and your wish to have her presence. Upon bringing her, she could see you at your craft and have her worries assuaged with art and story. You are well plied and versed in the role - that is unless you'd prefer to switch parts with me and play Pierre, which I would under the circumstance concede to."

Daniel thought a moment. "Why no, Merchant. With consideration of your idea, I would be proud to play Marco."

CHAPTER 17

Emily had waited and worried more of Daniel with each passing hour. She had just been considering walking the route back to Abigail's when there came a knock at the door. She remembered what Daniel had said about not answering it to anyone and was quiet, then suddenly heard the visitor speak outside.

"Daniel gives you greeting and invites you, Emily, to join him in the north. Well, you have done by your word not to open the door, but he asks that you make exception here. And so that you know whom I am, I am a fellow player from the theatre. My name is Kip." Emily looked at the door bemused, for just a moment, then went and opened it immediately.

"Hello Kip. Thou hast circumvented my berating mood of mind and assuaged my worries at the same. I will certainly, but why did not Daniel come to me?"

"He has practice and preparation of a sort which I should not divulge. It is of a good sort though. Shall we go," said Kip, and he motioned outside. "I have a capable horse at the ready."

"Yes, than. I am ready as well."

Kip and Emily rode back to the theatre for some distance. When they arrived, Kip hopped down and helped Emily to dismount. There was a crowd of people now outside and waiting at the front entrance into the theatre.

"Come," he said.

"Ah. My goodness. Is it as I think?" Emily started walking towards the crowd.

"Come; This way," said Kip, leading her to a side alley. "No need to wait." They entered through a side door that lead into a hallway. Emily followed Kip to a door that said 'Costumes and props' on it. They entered a large room packed with a wide variety of many different styles of clothing and items for the stage.

"I'm sure, you can find something to fit. Why not indulge; try the royal wears," said Kip with a wink. "Choose as you may though and make use of the dressing stalls, thence I will show you to the theatre." Kip smiled and went to wait outside and Emily began to browse through the racks of clothes.

Several minutes later, Emily stepped from the room in an embroidered blue and white dress in elegant yet simple style. Kip looked at her as though unsure what to say.

"How lookest I?" asked Emily.

Kip smiled. "My goodness," he mused. Emily smiled back at him.

"Shall we go?"

Kip brought Emily into the main theatre where people were just beginning to seat themselves. "Now, you may seat yourself as you choose; and enjoy the show miss. I assure you. You will see Daniel very soon."

Emily looked around with curious fascination. "Thank you. Thank you for coming to get me."

Kip bowed lightly then walked down the aisle to the stage where he climbed the stairs and walked in front of the closed curtain then slipped through an opening at stage left.

As Emily watched him do this, someone spoke beside her. "Excuse me. Are these seats still available?" Emily looked to her right where two young woman stood dressed in fine courtly dress.

"Yes. They are available."

The two young women sat down. "I thought, you might perhaps have a beau coming or such," said the nearest young woman.

"I have a beau somewhere about, but I believe he might be speaking for someone else today."

"Oh, my dear. I am sorry for you."

"No, no. Not for someone else's heart. For someone else's

character; 'pon the stage."

"Ah. 'Tis an artful discrepancy."

"I am much looking forward to it. I've never been the theatre. I have read plays but never seen them acted out."

The other young woman looked over to Emily. "You? I say. Why-ever not?"

Emily looked down. "Duties and more duties."

"Have you not a maidservant?" asked the first young woman.

Emily, for a moment had forgotten what image her new dress might well convey. She decided to enjoy the benefits of it and figured now was no time for confessions. "She is away; though were she here, I would give her, as always her six hours personal time per day, sick days, and Sundays off."

The young woman gave her a bit of an odd look. "'Tis generous of you."

"And only fair. My name is Emily. And yours?"

"I am Melissa," said the first young woman.

"And I am Guendoline," said the second.

"It is good to make your acquaintance."

"I have no beau presently, as my last I found in time, was inclined to strange habits and notions and 'twas apparent we were not a fit. I was with a young man yesterday named Darbey. He was nice enough, but -well... that may suffice," said Melissa.

"Mine is presently riding with his mates," said Guendoline.

"I can't recall having seen you about court," said Melissa looking at Emily.

"I have been residing in the Berkshires of late."

"Ah, you prefer the forested life," said Guendoline.

"I do enjoy the court as well."

"You should partake of it more. I and Melissa could take you around and make a day of it."

"I should like that," said Emily.

CHAPTER 18

Melissa, Guendoline, and Emily looked to the stage as the curtains began to open. The stage was covered in sand with a back drop of trees and distant Italian style architecture. Some makeshift hills were to the west side and a large blue blanket as the sea. Two men entered and walked east to west talking amongst themselves, dressed as field workers. The audience subsided from talking into quietness. Another man came walking by strumming a mandolin and exited the other side of the stage.

Another man came forward dressed in ragged looking clothes that looked like they were once fine garments. It was Merchant (In character as Pierre) who stood by the blue water and paced back and forth then looked out over the audience. He then turned and looked over the backdrop of scenery, shading his eyes from the sun. Emily smiled in the audience and her eyes lit up as the next actor came on stage. It was Daniel (In character as Marco) He approached Pierre with a bottle in his hand.

Pierre - Good day sir.
Marco - Mmmmhhh. The day has not good found me, but this makes better of't; So, to the day I'll drink of its temperate vineyard commodity, Quashed under foot.

Marco raises the bottle in his hand and drinks from it.

Pierre - Did it finish well?
Marco - Less punctuated than the start, but fuller all around. A fine petit Verdot. 'Twas but ten minutes hence, was't full; five minutes hence was't three quarter full; three minutes hence was...
Pierre - Are you going to tell me the emptying of a bottle?
Marco - Yes. That I may empty it again. Now where was I?
Pierre - At three minutes.
Marco - Oh yes, Three minutes and the cask is... blast it. I get no further Pleasure of it anymore.
Pierre - Words cannot be bottled and drunk in such particulate. 'Tis too much mixed chemistry. Take pleasure in speech for its content; not its alcohol content.

Marco - Art thou a puritan chemist?

Pierre - No. A ship wrecked traveler. My boat capsized in a storm and I swam unto this place. Would you tell me what island it is?

Marco - Sicily.

Pierre - Whence I lay on the shore in the sand, I thought I saw two nymphs singing at a fountain.

Marco - I drink and you see nymphs. Perhaps sea water is more the salt of your dram.

Pierre - No. 'Tis the sickness of my stomach. Why wouldst thou desire so much of a bottle?

Marco - 'Tis not my common practice. But, I have debts and it eases my worry.

Pierre - What was the cause of your debts?

Marco - A loan for a fishing boat. The boat sank and the shark circled, but being hungrier for a pound of currency than a pound of flesh, he thus sent collectors to ring the profits of carp out of me till I were a dry man. And after: still; as though the boat being at the bottom stead of top o' the water, were but the depths of my misfortune and none of his, nor any considerate factor of clemency in concern to the catch of his returns. Last I did happen upon him in the street earlier, he did gesture to me and I did run, marked by a pursuit from his yeoman, who was too round-about to catch me. Hence; I did come here to walk on the beach and think.

Pierre - How might I recognize him?

Marco - His name is Balfour. He has balding black hair that sits as matted hay 'pon his head; a thin mustachio, he sometimes wears gaudy rings and purple or white jeweled pumps on his feet.

Pierre - Well marked. The tussling of the sea has made me humble of nature and un-fearing of men. Should he poke his upturned nose at me, wave his questions and bill-fold or so much as tap my heel with his pumps, I will make a point of it; and if he should counter, than with something sharper yet.

Pierre grabs Marco's sword from its sheath and parries in the air.

Pierre - Come, you coxcomb scupper. Make me an offer.

Marco - Hast you not your own sword?

Pierre hands sword back to Marco.

Pierre - 'Tis as bottomed out as your fishing boat. It got away from me in the waves. I had clung to a plank of flotsam while they would swell like monsters and bear me up as though a cork, then heave me afore in a wash of swirling foam. 'Twas at the peak of one of these waves that I saw this island and with great effort amended my direction by turns between upheavals whilst clinging to my plank.

Marco - Thou art lucky, and we are marked - For look; a wench approaches. I say, her thighs can heave as well as any wave.

Pierre - Certainly sway. One could ride between to a sweet motion. I think we have both been too long without, and thinketh so, below the belt.

Marco - Yes. Though crudely, we may; she does walk this way.

-Enter-

Darlene - (Aside) Which one was it? The half tipsy gesticulator, or the inefficaciously fashionable wearer of fine rags. I will make inquest.

Marco - Miss. Do you tarry?

Darlene - I know how to; I think not by your persuasion though, but more, my own curiosity.

Marco - Of what?

Darlene - Such a strange pair.

Pierre - Why strange? We are but a pairing amongst many myriad of men, happened together.

Darlene - There are certain features of manner and accoutrements that are most typical to men of this place; none of which either of you possess.

Pierre - I will not ask what they are, for we do possess confidence in our own qualities, and I for one will not lean to affectations otherwise.

Marco - Nor I. Though I am of this place and know not what I am amiss of.

Pierre - I must say -and not to steal selfsame repeal- there is stranger fodder in the works with you than we, for your walk and look say one thing and your words, quite another.

Darlene - Appearances are more to affect anon and hither, whilst words have our privacy. What is your business here?

Marco - Business. What would you say our business is my friend?

Pierre - Perusal of options for me.

Marco - And my business is very willy-nilly for now, whilst I have that freedom. None too set upon terms or the hour or therewithal, but for my whim. And in-such; your company is sweet to it.

Darlene - Ah. You must a sweet tooth that chews a granule of sugar from something thou hast ate; for I've barely stroked a word of your ego nor flattered nor sighed nor told you intimacies, and have looked to you with question and skepticism.

Marco - But you have smiled and tempted with your beauty; and so: sweet to me.

Darlene - Is sweetness so disfigured? So half formed, to be but an outward thing?

Marco - To the eye, 'tis a taste for what-more?

Darlene - The eye should not speak so forwardly of that which is a given, rather than is given, until more willing sweetnesses are, thus.

Marco - I check myself. I have had some wine

Darlene - 'Tis well enough. I like familiarities to be earned, when business is not; for in business, they are taken and given so easily.

Pierre - Than, what is your business?

Darlene - Is't not obvious. For outwardly, you had observed. Though list my words and you may see it now, as a lark that lands at forty paces asunder. However; at another time, if you care to do business of the other sort...

Darlene flirts outwardly with Marco.

Pierre - Your words are odd. Does something trouble you?

Darlene - Where art thou from?

Pierre - I? France. Be troubled no more.

Marco - I am a native. No trouble.

Darlene - Than I will be forthcoming. I was paid to come over here and coerce the Sicilian salaciously. The man who paid me has come to the brothel and abused one of the women, so I have more issue with he, and now tell you of his intent to attend to you with violence just 'pon the cusp of yonder hill whence I was to bring you. I have my money. Now you have foresight of this, to do as you may.

Marco - I cannot deny here-upon, what is so willingly given. Thanks to you my sweet lady.

Marco takes her hand, kisses it and she smiles.

Pierre - What of you miss? I fear thou hast put thine self in danger.
Darlene - I think not. My part of the bargain looks kept to appearances; if you might do me favor.
Pierre - Speak it.
Darlene - We are three now. He would dare not act against us all. Might we walk hither together? Thence I have my money, your friend hath his safety for another day and you hast our gratitude.
Pierre - 'Tis well to me.
Marco - And I.

The three of them walk over towards the cusp of the hill. Upon reaching it, Balfour approaches them.
-Enter-

Pierre - Too brash. Too brash.
Balfour - (To Marco) Where's your carp money, my errant debtor? I saw you have enough to buy a bottle and a whore.
Pierre - Where's his boat you fool. Water log it in your records under acts of nature and give him clemency of time.
Balfour - This is none of your concern, sir. (To Darlene) And you wench. I said bring him alone.
Pierre - And she might walk with whom she pleases, as you might waste your money as you please.
Balfour - Be off. Dost thou hear? No business to you.
Pierre - Who are you to tell me my business? As I have heard - One: A stud with a cattle call of maids for his urges and beatings.

Balfour looks at him then puts his hand to his sword.

Pierre - Two: A pompous poof. - Oh, me, oh me, oh me. Be off saith he. -to your authority.

Flicking his fingers under his chin while Imitating his walk and talk.

Balfour - Draw you.

Pierre goes to Marco.

Pierre - May I?

Marco hands him his sword.

Pierre - Come you croaker scupper fop.

Balfour advances to him and after some swordplay and thrusts, Pierre counter-parries to a riposte and flicks the tip of his sword to his cap, sending it to the ground. He flinches at the closeness to his face.

Pierre - Three: A harbinger of death, who makes false epitaph and hires out the danger in the desperate.

Balfour comes at him again and they return thrusts and parry. Pierre then beats his sword away to the left with force and counter parries then in an instant thrusts his sword into Balfour's chest. He clutches his heart with a pained expression as blood colors and spreads at his white shirt. He drops his sword and falls to the ground as Marco and Darlene look on. Pierre watches him breath heavily, then his breath subside and his eyes go lifeless.

After standing there a moment, Pierre steps nearer to the dead man and looks over him as he begins to speak.

Pierre - What is a man's life, when a dancing sword can play with it? Alchemy of the cosmos, marked in some bloody self-made claim upon the blade? Then, the lingering eyes that tell of the afterward with solitary foresight, suggesting but a shadow for the living. The breath that was once so easy, vanquishing... till, in breath-the last: The leaving, as a mortal to the unknown. Then, heavy silence laced with equivocate of the exorcize that hangs about the senses and impregnates the air, and the still remains - a body; a savaged body, and no more. Therein doth the slayer search himself, all reason and moral deduction turning to portent or guile in the fathomless space of his skull.

Pierre falls to his knees and hangs his head.

The opening scene ended and the lights dimmed while the audience clapped and awaited the next scene.

Somewhere around the same time, the earl was packing for his vacation in his upstairs chamber. As he turned from his packing to retrieve something a large wild bird of some kind suddenly flew into his open window and jettisoned into the side of his head sending him to the floor. He got up in shock as the bird flew madly about the room.

"Headmistress! Headmistress!" he shouted. As she reached the upstairs and entered the room, the bird exited the window, though she did not see it. She looked at him with confusion. "Get out!" he finally barked. As the headmistress was leaving, she heard him get up. "Wait." She turned to him again as he looked at her with a disturbed expression. "Dost you know anyone by the name of Anne?"

The headmistress had anticipated the remote possibility of being asked this after the young maid had ran away. She looked at him with a blank confused look. "Why, no sir."

Merchant and Daniel were backstage after the opening act. "Thank you Merchant," said Daniel, "for coaxing me to it."

"My coaxing was but a reiterate for thine own desire" said Merchant.

"I noticed you did change some of the confrontation dialogue."

"Just somewhat," said Merchant. "I thought it appropriate," he said with a smile.

Daniel nodded and they hugged each other. The actor who was playing Balfour walked by.

"Did I poke yee a bit enthusiastically," asked Merchant.

"No mind. I shant complain of enthusiasm. T'only helps in affect, to feel it some." The actor removed his blood stained shirt and a small emptied blood packet pinned inside it. "How now. Good job Daniel. I was not expecting to see you in this."

"I am a last minute stand in Stefan."

Stefan hurried off to get into dress for a different character in the next scene. "Till next time Daniel. I must be brief."

"As you must. Till then."

Emily had much enjoyed watching the play. Especially in seeing Daniel up on stage.

"Which one was your beau?" asked Melissa next to her, with curiosity.

Emily looked to her. "He was Marco."

Emily, Melissa and Guendoline watched the remainder of the play until the final act some time later, when the actors took there bows and the curtain closed again. After a long ovation, they rose from their seats and began to leave the aisle with the rest of the crowd.

"'Twas delightful. I can't recall the story. It must be a new work," said Guendoline to her companions as they exited there row.

"It is new to us," replied Melissa.

Emily looked over to the stage as they were exiting and suddenly saw Daniel looking through the curtain and waving her over. "Oh my. Daniel beckons to me."

Melissa and Guendoline looked over as well.

"Would you care to come back stage as well?" Emily asked them.

Melissa smiled. "If you would have us to?"

"Most certainly. come, if you wish."

Melissa looked to Guendoline, who nodded with approval.

"Lead us the way than, Emily," said Melissa.

CHAPTER 19

Abigail began to wonder when Daniel might return, as it was now dark out. She was in the sitting room where she was looking through a book of maps and sketches of the Berkshires when a knock came at the door and she thought it would be him. Sara, who had been keeping her company, went to answer it. In a few moments she returned to the entrance of the sitting room.

"Miss Abigail. A man who says to be your father." Behind Sara came an old bearded man with a frail look.

"Father," Abigail emoted with a look of surprise.

The old man stepped slowly into the room and Sara left them to their privacy. "How so; as to the time, Abigail?"

"It has been long of it; and therewithal, the absence of you."

"Is this my predicate to it: A wide look, then casual note to the calendar of my neglect. Has it not been of matter to conjure moiety of parts that color absence more feelingly?"

"Do feelings of another, when left unattended to, nurture of themselves one day to the next. Such a lone prospect gleans anger, which I did foolish wage, then feverish, dissuade. Lack thereof, has paled them of a more natural complexion. And herein; expression is subdued."

"Yet, in that time, I have pondered the form and complexion of memory; the aspects of its place and affect with particulars of fondness - as to you, that now confer so presently, in the curve of your cheek, the upturn of your nose, your manner and movement that come into expression whence you give voice."

Abigail looked down with emotion. "Father. What has brought you?"

"I had word that you had taken injury from an assault."

"I have. I am on my way to wellness from it. Were it not for Daniel, it might well have been a different outcome."

"The boy is well?"

"He is no longer a boy father."

"No. I should say, the young man."

"He has been well. Though today, I am not so sure."

"My prejudices; my expectations have also been my grief, and I have learned through witness of their affect. Though I may never understand why thou choosest not to marry, whilst many a suitor would propose, I must accept your choice. I have found desire to o'ercome my own discomfit concerning the boy, and appreciate your gesture towards him. You must understand why it were so difficult for me. Whence I was to see him, it brought unpleasant events to mind again... Does he know?"

"He knows his mother was killed. Not how, or by whom." Abigail's father hung his head.

"How I still remember. 'Twere right where the Tayler River meets the Strike. The water was all a-spring rush. So loud, it was, that she probably could not hear the carriage approaching on the trail. Then; after the bend, all I recall is that moment as she tossed the babe into the woods just afore she went under the wheels."

"Oh father." She went to him and held his face. "'Twere an accident. Do not harbor it so long. As to him; he were but a babe at the time, and no more remembers the incident than his mother's face. He has heard of her, and has knowing that she was a good and honored lady. That is his ease and comfort."

"Yes. Yes than." Abigail's father sighed and she held him. "Shhh. Be well. Be well now," she said softly.

CHAPTER 20

Emily, Melissa, and Guendoline went through a curtained side door at stage right and into a dark hall. Emily followed the hall to a lighted area and climbed some stairs at the further end where she parted another curtain and saw Daniel standing with the other actors back stage.

She looked at him with relief and a glow of happiness. He came over to her, then lifted her up and hugged her.

"Know you not where my thoughts have been? What worry; what question?" chided Emily.

"Let it be passed, and know that I have held thee in my heart."

"I will than, for this gift to me -though it be the cause- has also been most pleasant answer to my unpleasant worries. How well it was to see you at your craft."

Emily turned to Melissa and Guendoline. "These are friends I met whilst waiting for the play to begin. Melissa and Guendoline;

this is Daniel."

"Pleased that you have come. Did thee, and thou enjoy the play?"

"'Twas funny then tragic," said Guendoline.

"Thence sadly funny," said Melissa.

"Thence imbued and resolved so in similar turns, till its auspicious conclusion," said Emily

"Parts had a more than common significance for me," said Daniel.

"Daniel," Merchant called from across the room, "a toast to the production at the Pig and Whistle?"

"What think you?" said Daniel to the three young women. They all nodded.

"Marco has put me of taste to it," said Guendoline.

"'Tis a well suggestion," answered Daniel to Merchant.

Daniel, Emily, Melissa, Guendoline, Merchant, Kip, and other cast members walked over to the Pig and Whistle Tavern down the street.

On the way over, Daniel walked behind alone with Emily. Emily could tell there was something else on his mind. "Emily. There is else I must tell you of this day. I had need await our privacy."

"What is't?"

"Whence I left this morn, I came upon Abigail on the trail where she had been accosted by some thieves. Thus, I had confrontation them."

Emily gasped. "What happened?"

"She is injured; but to no extent that shant be remedied by a goodly time of rest and care."

"And of you and the thieves?"

"I had do as I must."

Emily nodded her head and seemed to understand. "I am only most glad that you are well," she said, taking his arm.

They all entered the tavern. Inside the Pig and Whistle they sat at a row of tables and ordered drinks. When they all had their glasses, Merchant stood up.

"Think yee of a monk in a tunic walking past the lion's den of the Roman Coliseum, where the animal doth growl and paw and roar; all its fearsome bellow kept at bay by bars of iron - the prisoner in the next cell hearing it, awaiting his own blood to be spilled with limb rended from limb. Who is that monk? Whom is that prisoner? How to fathom within hairs breadth of its fearsome molded form, the lion? For, here is ours." Merchant slapped his hands against his chest. "Our minds reach and work; turn the wheels and form the syllables of expression and we act with motions picturesque. Many of us have chosen to put on that monk's tunic. Doth he perhaps conspire with angels, or hold them on his right shoulder whilst ignoring them on the left; or wear their images as amulets and regard them as mortally untenable and so live -in waiting- as a monk; or see Gods as works of art, mindful and mythic, mirrors to our own faces; or take them -as he may- a half spoon of sugar in his tea at night. To wear that prisoners garb and yell to Beelzebub in a corner, then whisper to oneself or wage wars with Gods and Devils in madness and cursed dreams. Perhaps he cares not a whit of such 'nonsense', but only to hammer his way through existence and fulfill his needs; or is it he perhaps who is more angel browed and wronged and the monk who walks by with a stiff gait of solitariness. It is these kinds of distinctions we work within on stage as in life. And the lion... well; any for the lion? say I." Laughter welled across the tables.

"I than," said a young slight actor with feigned timidity, and laughter erupted again.

"You'll need some practice. And so; thus and thus my speech will end, for these glasses and casks await. Just to say, you are my family in this and I did wish to acknowledge you for it. Wassail! Cheers to all."

Everyone gave response and drank from there cups.

Kip enthused, "The stage wast goodly set for storied speech; its temperaments, flourishes and footing. Did not thought erase plainer walls for visions? Did not the words find heartfelt acquaintance, travel, and share returns? Why, oft' sweetly, laughs did make their way, or gasps conceding to the act at hand from most becoming faces at a glance as therewith do sit across the table from me now," said Kip looking to the ladies.

Melissa smiled to Kip. "It is easy acknowledgement to earn for our pleasures sir."

"And welcome," added Guendoline.

"Especially that we were three in three hundred, and you involved as it were," said Emily.

"Never a job that keeps Kip from noticing pretty maids," said one of the actors.

"Though first -in such: as part, our dear audience." Kip said.

"Well; that you can do double duty so, and keep to't at both ends, why not? Careful as I'm sure you'll be of not going into some long multi-tempered soliloquy with patron maids in your head," Merchant pointed out.

"On stage, I take it as a lief gratification, as such; at the right time, and benefit the brevity of't more than the lingerance."

"And what if a lady of that letter sits across from you later, and -sans play- your thoughts do linger?" asked Melissa.

"Than I know I am not on stage anymore, and she is worth remembering."

"Well Kip," she replied, "what is to be done then?"

Kip looked at her speechless for a moment and the others laughed. "That which one would. Though it may be quicker than thought," said Kip musingly.

"Here is a thought, Kip," said Melissa, as she reached her hand to him across the table. He leaned across and kissed it.

"Oh. He is quick now," said Daniel and everyone laughed.

"Quick as a blush," said another actor.

"Daniel," said Merchant. "I hope you might be more regular to our productions now; from the pleasure Emily got of it, you might just find encouragement from her in that,"

"Oh, I will encourage," said Emily, "For I cannot do without now, and were he not on the stage, I should expect him to be seated next me, thence restless to the effect in having to only watch."

"I will keep in touch. Mark my word," said Daniel. He turned and spoke with Emily more quietly as the others talked. "What didst thou do whilst I was away?"

"I did take interest in your writings and sketches 'pon the table. I hope thus was not too improper."

"I said to do as comforts thee."

"Thence I did put a chair here and a table there, for the chair was hampered to its purpose by a cramped space and the table had not enough light; seeing as they are both quite moveable -to your taste, as to mine."

"I shall give them the benefit of your taste than and be reminded you, in the arrangement."

"Thence, this and that and the other of small consequence; more inclined to thought and reflection as I was; in prior of worries," Emily said touching his arm.

Two of the other actors down the table were talking with one another of something one of them had seen recently:

"...Thence the queens carriage had stopped, adjacent the market whence a yeoman emerged. 'Pon walking over to this merchant and asking something, the merchant scooped up a mackerel from a tub and flapping in his hand, wrapped it alive thence and there (an impressively slippery task) and wouldst hand it to him. The yeoman looked at him first as a madman thence with contempt at the action being some sort of fishy jibe at the monarchy, whilst the fish flapped as best it could in a bundle. 'Wouldst thou wish it dead, before handing over sir.' Will take but a minute or so of wait time; consider a death o' the air as more genteel than the pummeling of't. Look; it gasps already. 'Tis a fish-impeccable and untampered, for porcelain and the jabs of silver forks,' said he. The fish having died, the yeoman reluctant to make issue, took it and left. Some who watched said the shop-keep had a brother beaten and hanged for theft and something or other and his bitterness took on some meaning in the strange act."

Stefan (from the play scene) and another actor sat together and talked at the other end of the table.

"A cobbler did approach me yesterday about my shoes. He said they looked a little wearened about the heel and could put on new soles for a sixpence."

"Did you take him up on't?"

"Nay. I told him he was a brash cobbler to try and drum up business accosting people in the street on condition of their shoes; though I did examine them thereafter and confer. I may go his shop and sooth the indictment with recognition of his observation and have the matter (with temperaments allowing) evened out as it were into some business."

And Kip talked with Melissa whenever he could get a chance across the table in the loud and busy tavern.

The night changed to late-night. Daniel, Emily, Merchant, Kip, Guendoline and Melissa left soon and some of the other actors stayed longer.

"Must needs you Daniel and Emily, room and bed?" asked Merchant.

"We could ride back to the Berkshires."

"Now? You would not see a foot in front of you."

"I have as such -a ladies bed," said Guendoline. "For my father would not have a man -though he be gentleman- sleeping over by my charge."

"'Tis my pleasure to accept," said Emily.

"And Melissa. I would not see you making home at this hour, so your pillow is boded for as well."

"I have need to change," Melissa sighed.

"How so?" said Guendoline. "I like thee as thou art."

"No. Clothes."

"Ah; These. We are much of the same proportion. I could lend you one of my dresses."

Melissa smiled. "Very well than."

"Thus leaves you Daniel, and a cot doth for a bed make; and Kip is Kip," said Merchant.

"Aye. As my bed, is a bed not needed in-stead," said Kip

"Than be we sleepy-heads for a spell," said Daniel.

Merchant considered. "Let us meet at the theatre sometime of the morn."

"Be not expecting us too early," said Guendoline, "as I for one desire a good sound rest."

"As you may," said Merchant.

"Than it is decided," said Emily.

Daniel went with Merchant, Emily and Melissa went with Guendoline, and Kip walked home thinking of Melissa.

Abigail insisted her father take a chamber and sleep at her residence as it was too dark to ride home through the Berkshires, then he could take leave in the morning. After showing him to his room, she went to read her book again where she fell asleep on the long sofa.

And so, the day ended.

CHAPTER 21

Melissa awoke early the next morning with sun dawning in the window and opened her eyes out of half sleep. "Papa. Why didst thou move the window?" she murmured. She roused herself, then looked around remembering she was still not at home. She looked to her left where Emily slept in a second bed. Emily lay facing the other way and Melissa wondered if she were awake yet. She began to sing quietly:

Deery aye-O day, art thou awake?
deery Aye-O lee, could'st answer to me.

Emily sang in reply:

Falal-O the day, to answer, I may,
falal- O the lee, no more do I sleep.

Emily turned to her and smiled. "Didst thou sleep well?" asked Melissa.
"'Tis the most comforting bed I ever did lay long enough to close mine eyes."
"Truly?" said Melissa curiously.
"I am more accustomed to straw mats and such."
"Why-ever so?"

Emily looked down. "I must confess something. The truth be, I am a maid."

Melissa laughed. "Why, of course you are."

"You misunderstand. In most literal terms; I am, or was, a maidservant."

"You do not look as a maidservant. I think thou hast outdone thy place and become quite something else."

"I know of a certain earl who would have me punished as such, were he to get his hands on me."

"Oh really? Perhaps this earl needs a talking to and to be put in his place, and I would be one to do so."

"You are most kind Melissa, but I prefer to let time have its sway, to quell the hot indictment with the passage of days and this and that concern till it might change to the afterthought; thence… fade into recollect of the mind. There, naught or lesser troubles are stirred, for some are provoked and made craftier by confront."

"And yet, some hold slights, as they hold eyes in there head."

"Though his, more the precursor to mine."

"All the more reason than."

"But herein, wouldst come the truth to the fore: when with time's reflection and pricks of awareness (for some darts are too swift for the trained rebuffing mind) might his eyes come to see thus; lest that mind hath been helmed so cunningly that truths be made lies or pernicious play things. By some observation, do I regard him not so resignedly ignoble."

Melissa nodded. "Than let him be; and be not our topic."

"I am prone to another topic, that should not lay so long," said Emily.

"As I. So I will say't. From bed, from bed! Come. Let's go rouse Guendoline. If habit concedes, than she'll still be a-slumbering, and change is a puckish soothsayer to habit; to break it with a rousing good morn!"

"Than, let it not be a thought to sleep on."

They both got up and went down the hall to Guendoline's room to wake her.

Melissa entered Guendoline's room first and jumped with enthusiasm to the foot of her bed. "Good morning to you," she intoned in sing song voice.

Guendoline stirred and half looked through bleary eyes, then put her head back down.

Emily jumped lithely to the other side of her bed. "With song and with woo," she added in sing song as well.

Guendoline stirred again and mused "What kind of morning larks are you two? I beseech. Sleep still lends me the pillow." Guendoline curled to it.

Melissa stepped closer. "Than let me steal it and sleep will leave in a huff." She pulled the pillow gently from Guendoline's clutching hands.

Guendoline sat up in a fluster and rubbed her eyes. "Oh. You intrepid sprites!" She grabbed the second pillow on her left and swung it at Melissa who yelled and ducked away. "Come, pillow stealers. If not sleep, than this." She jumped up and swung at Emily as well and Emily ducked and laughed, then Melissa hit Guendoline in the thighs and the pillow burst and feathers exploded into the air around them. Guendoline stood a moment in shock, then hit her back and her pillow exploded as well.

Daniel and Merchant had awoken and were about to head back to the theatre. Daniel was looking from the window of Merchant's flat where he could see the Tayler River at a distance. There was a ship at the port docks that passengers were boarding. One of those passengers was to be the Earl of Bale.

Merchant entered the room. "Let us hither?"

"Yes."

They both walked down to the street and towards the theatre.

"Anon, the bell strikes nine. There are the shop-keeps putting out their wares. Anything to be had Daniel?"

"Thus I would buy -for a thought- parchment. Ideas have come to me thence -to make me a barker. 'Tis those most pretty slender trees I seek out that peel in pinions of white, streaked and crannied, that whence turned over show a most contrasting smooth cream surface to write upon. They do well, but alas, I am stripping the poor birches so that they might -if they could- resent that I pick up a quill."

"I know a shop." Merchant and Daniel passed a drunk rolling over and groaning in an alley.

"This drunkard rolls in his stone bed and holds his head to a rude awaking of pains."

"As are begotten of devil-may-care drink, having been roused in the blood with a churlish kind of complicity. Here we are." Merchant pointed out the shop and They went inside to look around.

"I will pick my parchment. Look you for else?"

"A new stage marker."

They found their items and went to the counter.

"Ay. Mornin men. Had you anything else to acquire?" checked the shop-keep.

"Nay sir. We are made well to our needs."

"Than, parchment and marker make for three pence." Daniel paid for the items and they left.

After walking a few streets, they stopped into another shop that Merchant suggested. An old man came out from a back room. "Here is Merchant and Daniel. Come to visit the old tinkerer."

"Hardly a tinkerer Marilius. Good to see thee. He has been fashioning a timepiece in miniature," said Merchant to Daniel.

"A fashion of the weighted time tone device or the water clock?" asked Daniel.

"Nay. Its properties of time-keeping are similar to the tower clock in the workings, and also fashioned as the sundial without the necessity of adhering to true north and correct latitude. It came about by accident as it were. I was commissioned to design a clock for the tower by the Arms and Laws quarter. Upon fashioning a model in miniature to work with I began to perceive the possibility of this model itself being feasible. It might precede the tower clock, for its small size is in proportion to its labor. For descriptive purposes, think you of the miller's wheel: The buffeting of the water that doth turn the wheel and the beam; thus the cogs of the machinery. Now imagine that wheel in the form of an affixed pin the size of your smallest fingernail, and all parts thus re-proportioned, fit onto a compressed spheres flat surface. As tension and energy is produced by the water to the wheel of a mill, here, 'tis produced by the turning of this pin thus affecting springs and tensions, which are transferred to a cyclical component in the form of a single marker —as is seen on tower clocks and the like, or is similarly and naturally ascribed pon the face of the sundial- that turns out the passage of time and follows it through the prevailing system of numbers situated evenly about the circumference of the circle. Thus, one hour passing observed and marked -as from the point of noon to… but, this you already know."

"Fascinating. Dost you have a working model?"

"'Tis not perfectly done as of yet."

"Such finely wrought work would bare its breadth of labors and ambitions in its stages of imperfection."

"Wait thus. I will retrieve a working model."

Marilius went behind a curtain then returned a moment later with his watch which he showed to them.

"Here is the turning of the wheel, and store of energy," said Marilius while winding the pin on the side.

They all watched the marker begin to move unevenly about the face of the watch with fascination.

"Amazing," said Daniel.

"The design owes as much to the metallurgists and smelters advances and the minute detail in the forgers work, as it doth the findings of astronomers, mathematicians, and numerologists that have laid out the means and processes of tracking time for us, that we may watch and observe it —now- on this compressed sphere, near the size of a three pence piece."

"If it might be within my means, I should like to obtain one, when you have completed models," Merchant said.

"You are on a short list as of yet, Merchant, which may not be for long."

"Than, we shall leave you to your work. My thanks for showing us the piece, but first, I must ask. How fares your daughter Marilius?"

The old man hung his head. "Alack; little has changed."

"My best wishes to her as always."

Marilius nodded.

"Fare thee well Marilius," said Daniel.

"Daniel, Merchant, Come again."

Merchant and Daniel left and continued to the playhouse.
"I abstained from issue of thought for his daughter, as I know not
what pertains, and thus observing such a pall come over his face at
the mention of her, thought better than to question further,"
Daniel explained.

"She hath taken on a malady of some sort that causes her fits
and turns of nature. The old man did divulge so much to me, but
grows quiet at further talk of't. I can see how it has taxed him,
though. I think there is good medicine for him in his work and
invention, long as he can give his mind to it for a deserved time.
Come; to the theatre now."

Melissa, Emily, and Guendoline had come downstairs then gone to
the parlor room to accustom themselves to the day a little before
heading to the theatre. They sat in some arm chairs.

"Where be your father?" asked Melissa to Guendoline.

"He is upon visit for a week or so with some lord who has some
common interests. I just hope the man's son is not one of these -
taken up in my honor- for I will not honor he with my interest. I
care not for him, though my father has had care to mention him
several times. I thought my decision not to attend with him were
hint enough."

"Your father did not protest?"

"Oh, some. He knows how hard I am to crack when it comes to
such personal fare; and were he to prevail, it would come to me
being dragged there in a distemperate mood. I could not help than,
but to find some means of having it out with the poor boy in some
way or other -truth be known- for I detest forced intimacies. I am
glad I stayed with my two friends."

"Though you had planned on learning the flute today."

"Oh, that. Sometimes ideas need time to savor of themselves. I
do like the flute, but - you know how it went."

"Melissa play's the harpsichord nicely," Guendoline said to
Emily.

"Ah. I have heard them. So pretty."

"Whence I play, a pigeon is soon to be at my sill."

"They like your playing?"

"Well; not they, as it is only one, so it may be that music from home is music for he. 'Tis a trained pigeon."

"For sooth," Emily said. "Could it be? Dost go by the name of Percy?"

Melissa looked at her shocked. "However dost thee know of a secret messenger bird?"

"By a lady named Abigail."

"Here is coincidence," Melissa said in her surprise.

"She is of recent acquaint to me; a dearest friend to Daniel."

"How our paths have crossed before we know it. I shall write her of our meeting."

"Do."

"A secret messenger bird?" Guendoline said in query.

"That of letters writ' and put to wing one window to another."

"Oh. How fascinating. Could he come here?"

"There are only two peopled homes, fit in his heart. Wither else he may go, is but on bird business that we not know."

"He is envied, I would say. I had read of recent in the monitor - this: That a man had constructed a configuration of wood and taffeta wings worn about the back and flapped by pullies and ropes."

"Did he get far?" asked Emily.

"No farther than Icarus -but for the sun- though being unmortalled (as he was) he might, as likened a bird, gone afar."

"That is an angel-thought," said Emily.

Guendoline shrugged. "Or just a thought with wings."

"What thought to angel, or winged thing?" mused Melissa.

"Come. Should we to the theatre now?" Guendoline suggested.

"Let's," said Emily.

Melissa nodded agreement.

Daniel and Merchant already at the playhouse were readying some props for an upcoming show. Merchant looked over at Daniel curiously as they worked.

"Durst your thoughts find better acquiescence?"

Daniel looked up. "More so. Much more so, Merchant."

"I will not seek to influence -there, that she may- but to say; you and Emily together, make for a most becoming picture."

Daniel smiled to him, then looked down in thought.

A few moments later, Merchant and Daniel looked up the aisle as they heard someone enter the foyer and come into the theatre. A woman stood there and looked at them.

"Marianna," Daniel said with surprise.

"Is't all in a name; that sweetness withheld? -To my seeming ears. 'Twere that it fell in repute by a jaded tongue of last, and thence I did fast so feverishly 'pon the heart's aching. But mark me not; for 'twere the premise of a dissolute spell. Here - I have a smile. 'Twere kept of a sickness that passed a while."

"What brings you?" asked Merchant.

"Drama Merchant! Pangs and turn of thought; what is, for what is not; fickle impressions, thence, wrong bedfellows and curses. Be it not for the stage, but more seasoned ears to scenes of another sort." Marianna stepped onto the seat backs and jumped lithely from one row to the next in an acrobatic balance to the front aisle by the stage. She hopped down in front of them and bent backwards putting her hands on the stage and looking at them. "And the dancer looks upside-down. Does her smile show a frown?" Marianna righted herself and put her chin in her hands with elbows on the stage. "'Twould ache for something. Daniel; what is something?"

"Nothing that I can know, but to accomplice with you to unreasoning."

"I wouldst that you would leave," said Merchant.

"Merchant. You already did give me my leave. Shun me a second time upon a simple visit and I would take affront."

"You, Affront? Were it that I took affront when thoust made chaos of my theatre productions, to make one take leave and drive another to the madhouse. That I finally had enough sense to let you go was the result of my affront."

"The mad to the madhouse, as it were. And Daniel; didst thou take leave for me? I wouldst to know."

"Not for thee. For the sake of the production."

"And what of me? Were my heart not warranting adieu?"

"Dost thou forget?"

"Forget, forget me nots? be't not. Wouldst thou hang a flower for my heartache in secret, or do I forget? 'Twere but a peevish spell that made the sweet, to rot. Oh. Let me cut of its bad parts." Marianna took a knife from her sleeve and jabbed it softly against her chest. "Deceitful heart. For shame. Here is the gardener."

"Marianna! No!" shouted Daniel.

Marianna held the knife to her chest then pulled back the front of her dress to reveal a silver necklace she wore with a medallion on it. She smiled and slid the knife down against it breaking it from her neck and it fell to the floor. She picked it up and threw it on the stage.

"There is unspoken promise, fashioned as a trinket, worn in faith of good time; now, an empty design. And for remembrance? A sigh and a cry. What to that? - here am I. Sweetness? Doth fade so - sweetness? Alack. I am more for the cold."

Marianna turned and walked from the theatre and Daniel hung his head and left the stage.

Emily, Melissa, and Guendoline had left for the theatre. Sometime later, they came in through the front doors of the playhouse and crossed the foyer into the main entrance. Emily looked around then finally saw Merchant sitting despondent in one of the theatre seats. She walked over to him.

"Merchant. What bodes so heavily?"

"'Tis but the ailments of the past."

"Is there medicine?"

"That for he, wouldst be for me."

"Daniel?"

Merchant nodded.

"Where than is he?"

"Behind the curtain."

Emily went to the back of the stage and behind the curtain and found Daniel sitting in thought.

"Would your thoughts - to words, for me?"

"They are thoughts of the past that closure had lacked."

"Were they sheish of nature?"

"So they were; but most troubled in persuasion."

"Is trouble for she, trouble for we?"

"Be it not, but for this reflective spell, that deduces wellness, from wan; and in knowing - thereto, it may soon go." Daniel sighed then smiled to Emily.

"Than, for a time, let me honor reflection," said Emily and she smiled to him. Emily stood silently for a moment. "Oh, I need return this wardrobe to its rightful place," she said suddenly with a lighter air, and she went to the props room to give Daniel some time and to change back into her own dress.

PART THREE- BACK TO THE FOREST

CHAPTER 22

Emily came out from the costumes room with her cotton dress on a short time later and sat across from Daniel in the quiet hall. She looked at him silently for several moments.

"Thus I see and thus I find, in sole delight, my heart and mind. Is't selfishness that colors me, with gentle hand and rosy cheek? For here your hand and cheek as well, before a word can even tell, my fingers know, mine eyes can see, most well when I'm alone with thee."

Daniel looked down reluctantly. "Do not our hands and cheeks dream some?"

"Than do we; for they are ours. If this be dreaming, than let my life be a living dream, and the rest of it, what it may. Why do you take umbrage thus and look to doubt? For it dotes on the heart with cruel ploys of reason."

"So it has reasoned with me, and I cannot disregard its cruel issue; I must recognize the issue as my own -to a fault. That which hath been, and that of who I am doth rub in this. This cheek has also blushed with heat of duress and brought blood to this hand. Know you of its more fair colors; but not beyond the pale."

"And have I not blushed at times to my own acts? And would my heart flinch that you have drawn an arrow in these troubled times? I would hang its happiness on the reason behind it, and remind it of my beloved's courage to give ponder and regard to the sanctity of life whilst countless others hath swung their swords and dulled their mind to the act with hardened eyes and faces. I know of your duties and that place in your heart where the woods nurture with a solitary way. Be this as much in my heart as yours, that I may honor its aspect as part of my beloved and his life."

Daniel thought then took Emily's hand. "That your words find devotion in these matters, with consort and gesture that I would to appease, does aware me of entertaining them so selfishly, where they did feed on their own misgiving. Therefore -sweetest companion- I know of a short walk. 'Tis an aisle, so is said. A pastor stands at the end of it."

"Does he?" Emily said with glowing excitement. "Than let him speak. But first, you."

Daniel knelt down before her and took her hand. "Emily. Wouldst thou marry me?"

"Yes I will."

Melissa and Guendoline stood outside the theatre, where Melissa decided to hail a coach for home. They were standing and waiting for one when Daniel and Emily came back out together.

"Daniel and Emily. Are you off now?" asked Melissa.

"Yes, we be."

Guendoline looked at Emily curiously. "Emily. My; 'tis a sully to dressmakers that here you stand, in -may I step lightly- cloth that might be garnered so plainly in appeal, yet you wear so radiantly, as to outdo such fine garb as you had on just of recent."

"I could wear a sack and be as radiant as the sun, for if clothes make the woman, than fashion is fickle in my favor, and if a woman make the clothes, than call me a dress maker, for I will wear it with a smile."

"Prithee; that I might know the secret," asked Guendoline.

"'Tis one of hands," said Emily.

Guendoline and Melissa thought and looked at their friends holding hands.

"They do not sew thought as to dresses," said Guendoline musingly.

"As they are, we shall be."

"Oh! Joined!" Enthused Melissa.

Guendoline and Melissa both hugged her and Daniel and gave them congratulations.

CHAPTER 23

Jasper was on board the ship where he'd been hired on. He was gathering up the rigging rope and tidying the deck. While he was doing this, passengers passed along the walkway of the ship and looked about. It was after a few moments that one man came and stood at the railing looking out at the water. He watched him with growing awareness. Most passengers were in there cabins or the commons room and after a few more couples passed it was just he and the man (The Earl of Bale) standing ten paces apart. Jasper rose to his feet, his heart thumping. He knew all it would take is one good push and he would be over and gone in an instant, never to be seen again. He walked towards him as though teetering on a precipice himself and heard in his head, his dead partner's words. 'Eiel get what's comin to em.' Jasper slowed his pace and raised his hands for a moment then did not stop, but continued walking past as the trembling in his chest subsided. He went to his cabin and sat down to think and realized it was Bernard he had hated at that moment he decided not to push the Earl. As he hadn't been able to do in life, he defied his words in death. It was the robbery that had bothered him most, and his remembrance of the woman they had harmed.

CHAPTER 24

Francis Riley was at that time, making his way to the Royal Palace for his appointment with Lady Michelle in consideration of the portraiture they'd spoken about. He walked the length of Southmark Road from the Brolen Region to the Royal Court, wanting to have time to consider the technique and placement he might use for all possible situations he could conceive of happening, though during the walk, he often found himself thinking on philosophy and theology as he had been reading on of late. He wore his easel and painting supplies attached to a shoulder harness that was slung over his back. As Francis neared the royal guards at the draw to the palace, he withdrew his invite and readied it for them to look over.

"Approach you sir; to what purpose?" asked the guard steadily.

"'Tis of outline, herein. To concur with't, I am being interviewed for consideration towards commission of a portraiture on behalf of Lady Michelle, at her request."

The guard looked over the document, then handed it back to Francis. "Follow this mark. He will lead you therewith to the chamber which is to be employed for the service."

"Well and good."

Francis followed his mark down a series of hallways into the palace. He looked with awe upon tapestries and treasures from across oceans and civilizations that decorated the rooms they passed through. The mark's footsteps echoed sharply as they strode further into the palace until coming to a stop at a large double sided door. The mark then gave three swift raps upon the door, at which point when no-one answered, he entered.

"Lady Michelle and company shall in time be present. I have been instructed to give you entry and lock the door upon leave. For your wait, there is wine," said the mark. He then turned and exited, locking Francis within the room. He was somewhat nonplussed at being interred within the room, but glad to have wine. He poured himself a glass straight away. Francis was there for some time, and filled and refilled his glass till he'd thought to have emptied what seemed the contents of the bottle, when at last he heard footsteps outside the door and he looked up as the door was opened.

There stood Lady Michelle whom he had met previously in the royal garden, and a young woman with short blonde hair, whom he assumed to be his subject.

"This is my confidante," said Lady Michelle. Francis found it an odd way to introduce her, but decided it was out of their desire for privacies.

"A pleasure." He bowed lightly to her.

"And Lady Michelle. Well to see you again." He bowed to her as well.

The confidante looked at him with lucid blue eyes. Her close cropped blonde hair might have lent her a boyish quality, but for a certain feminine beauty which made her appear ambiguous in nature; a young woman who seemed not quite a young woman - but something other than boyish.

"I am Francis Riley," he said, decidedly determined not to let the alcohol influence his behavior or affect this opportunity.

The confidante smiled. "Hast thou brought samples?" she inquired.

"Yes," said Francis. He slid off his harness then removed some rolled up canvases from inside it. He unrolled them and laid them out on the pedestal table, by which Lady Michelle and her friend sat down. The confidante perused over them for a moment.

"An eye to the subject, as much as the technique; Verily." She looked up at him. Francis met her inquisitive eyes, then she took a moment to wander about the room. "Of thine way here, didst thou see hither, the maypole?"

"Ay; that it was, being hoisted apropos."

"'Tween these summery days," the confidante said musingly while looking from the arched window. "It doth hold fond memories, of note. Keen steps and darting eyes, wistful impetuous smiles, and ancient rhymes. Now, some would have it marked by a symbol of the cross. Sanctus Spiritos Factitious. Doth flourish of late; this Christianity."

"It has, I would say."

"Dost thou partake of it?"

"By catches, by turns. Not as a practice. For it highs to the low, and lows to the high for me, to make a craned neck for a dour foot, that I should wonder why -are truths so grave? Is't that I am so uncouth?"

The confidante smiled to him. "Nay Francis. There are many Gods about the sun, in the image of man's usurped believing -that the weather can be waylay in such godly made planets reign."

"Than, is God the sum of all thought?"

"As much as you are the thought of some God."

"Which one?" asked Francis.

"The one that goes by any name," the confidante whispered, then she looked away.

Francis rubbed his eyes as Lady Michelle came and refilled his glass of wine from another bottle.

"Why, thank you, good lady."

She acknowledged with a nod then went and sat on a chair by the window, pouring a glass for herself as well.

"Where is your friend from the gardens?" he asked of Lady Michelle.

"In some ladies bed I would imagine."

Francis looked at both the young women, silent for a moment.

"A Portraiture?" Lady Michelle suddenly said keenly.

"What say you?" asked the confidante of Francis.

"For certain. I am at your service."

He rose to his feet and prepared his easel in a corner of the room as the young woman went and stood by the window. Lady Michelle fixed her hair and helped her finesse her pose then went to a small bureau across the room. To Francis astonishment she took a thin letter opener from the drawer with her right hand and a frog with her left. Lady Michelle brought the letter opener and frog to her confidante and she took them from her, as Francis watched curiously.

"I will thus, begin than," he said with a strangeness of voice. As Francis began to make an initial pencil sketch of his subject, the frog which she'd been holding began to creep slowly up her hand and wrist then into the sleeve of her dress and up her arm.

"Are you well?" asked the confidante looking at Francis with concern.

"Should you care to retrieve the frog, I can wait," he replied after a moment.

"The frog?"

The confidante looked down, and after glimpsing a slight movement, suddenly jabbed the letter opener to her breast. Francis yelled then saw her tear the bloody skewered frog from between the buttons of her dress.

The confidante held it up and gave the dying reptile a glance then lowered the letter opener with its victim to her side. She then looked to Francis. "I feel you need a remission."

"Remission?" repeated Francis bemused.

"Absolution?" Lady Michelle said, and he looked at her strangely, his thoughts spinning.

"Yes," he said, stepping weakly away from his easel. "I may." Francis fell dizzy into the chair at the pedestal table then held his head in his hands.

"Is this Devil's work?" He drew in a breath, unsure if he had said the words out loud or just thought them.

"Whom?" said the confidante suddenly, and Francis threw up his head, noticing her dress was now unstained, and the skewered frog was gone, but the letter opener was still in her hand.

"Yea, that we may know better than to follow a God, coerced. Now, there is more than a Devil's rite. There is in this world, strange fruit as would drop from heaven to hell. In the chambers of these halls hath I known of a lady awoken to cloth tied about her wrists, the Devil at the foot of her bed. There wouldst any say, is evil. But lo, I say; there is man trying to break the back of nature. Evil is man's invent, and it may fashion thee in its image if thou nurture it as food for thought -a malformation of the senses that any sensible Devil would not have, so as to have some wits about him. The Devil may exist, if you should deem it so, as Gods may exist as you deem them so, and therewith, may they go by, or under, any guise or form as is fit! There is better stuff than Devils to be made; and there is better truth than prophets to be followed! Know thine self."

Lady Michelle suddenly threw her wine glass across the room and it shattered into pieces against the mirror.

All was quiet for a moment. Francis pondered her action, and the confidante's words and he could feel his senses swirling in his head as though stirred by his confused thoughts. He massaged his eyes then looked to Lady Michelle then her confidante and thought he saw her wink.

"Were this but common wine...?"

Francis held his head in his hands and let out a groan, then heard shuffling sounds across from him. He shook himself and looked up again as if in a daze, but instead he found himself tumbling once over and looking across the floor at a vertical angle to the aperture window, and with another shake of his head, realized he had fallen, and the chair (his own) -now laying across from him on the floor- had done the shuffling as it slid out from under him.

"Dear God," Francis exclaimed getting up to his feet and brushing down his vest and pants. He looked around at the empty room for a few moments, breathing heavily, then he picked up his fallen chair and sat down again by the pedestal table to calm himself. After a few moments, he went over to the wine bottle on the floor and picked it up then put it into the casement across the room at the back of the bottom shelf. He picked up his easel and shoulder harness which also lay on the floor, leaning them against the wall. He then walked around the room for a few moments to clear his head, before sitting down to await Lady Michelle and her charge.

After a time, Francis heard footsteps outside the door and looked across the room as the door opened.

There stood Lady Michelle from the royal garden and -to his specific notice- not a young short haired blond woman, but a young lady with long chestnut hair and a delicate smile.
Francis bowed to them. "My ladies."

"I am sorry sir," said the lady. "We were detained, longer than expected. Did the mark provide you some wine as I asked?"

"Yes m'lady. 'Twas very good of you."

"As a sign of thanks for your waited internment."
Francis nodded.

"We were at the May day festivities since early morn and the dances were so wistful and light with mirth that we did stay of many hour."

"Oh. Such is a fine pretext to my waiting, as any; to be sure."

"I am glad you could come," said the lady. "Hast you brought some examples of your work?"

"Yes," said Francis, and he went to retrieve them, feeling a kind of deja-vu as the two young women sat around the pedestal table. Francis removed the canvases from his bag and laid them out in front of the young woman and Lady Michelle.

"A keen eye," she said softly. "Very good. Shall we have a session?"

Francis smiled. "Yes. I am at your service."

He rose to his feet and prepared his easel in a corner of the room as the young woman went and stood by a royal emblem on the wall. Lady Michelle fixed her hair and helped her finesse her pose then removed a small letter opener and a letter from a pocket of her dress, then handed them to her. Lady Michelle then went and sat by the pedestal table.

"I wish," said the young woman, "to have the sketch-mark 'pon this letter portrayed clearly, as such." She dangled the letter artfully from her left hand so that the sketch (a simply drawn flower in the upper right corner) would be visible to Francis.

"May I acquire closer observance?"

"Do."

Francis stepped forward and studied the sketch. "Mmmhh; easily done." He returned to his easel. Francis had without wanting to, wondered what the letter was, or whose it was? He noticed his heart begin to beat a little faster at several vague notions in his head, and tried to put the thoughts out of his mind by mixing colors on his easel before looking up at the young woman again to start an initial sketch. She was looking at him very succinctly now.

"Matters of the monarchy are very complicated Francis, and to be kept private. Do we understand each other?"

Francis stepped from his easel and bowed to her across the room. "Most certainly, m'lady."

She softly twirled the letter opener a few times in her right hand, then settled into a studied complexion and pose as Francis began to sketch an initial drawing.

CHAPTER 25

Daniel and Emily had mounted their horse outside the theatre and began the ride back into the Berkshires and the return trip to Abigail's.

Meanwhile, Nemo had left the Berisfurd's estate and gone out on another errand through the Berkshires. As he was walking in the woods he began to sing a song he knew:

Robin is gone
but bear is somewhere in the trees
Robin is gone
but possum comes for tea

The mushroom is tall
and it looks so good to eat
the mushroom is tall
by measure of others I've seen

So I'll go and chop it over
bring it home over my shoulder

Don't take too long
or briar fox will come round again
don't take too long
or I'll be sitting on a fence

Robin is gone
but possum comes from down a hole
Robin is gone
and maybe possum knows.

Sometime later, after entering a glade, Nemo saw two people approaching on horseback from the other side. As they neared, he realized it was the young woman and the man with the bow that he'd seen separately the other day. They both looked to him and recognized him as well and the young man at the reins brought the horse to a canter and they came over to him.

"How now friend?" said Daniel.
"Well to see you. Thou art a good apple splitter."
"'Tis but a trick. They are better to eat," said Daniel.
"And miss; didst thou find employment?"
"Much of it; though not in the maid services."
"Very good, very good," said Nemo.
"I see thou art much a wanderer of the woods, as myself," observed Daniel.
"Yes. I do enjoy it. I have my errands and outings."
"Are you off on one of them now?"
"Ay. To get some supplies and such."
"I thought to hear sweet tenor, trills and warbles from afar. You do voice it well."
"'Tis pleasant past time. Out here, I can do so freely."
"Wouldst thou sing us one away?"
"Certainly."
"I shall leave slowly. Adieu, my friend."
Nemo waved then began to sing again:

Once, a sweet maid she did come to me, too-
ra lye ay, too-ra lye eee,
as pretty as any I ever did see,
too- ra lye ay, too-ra lye eee,

come yee and go yee as you may do,
but once that a sweet maid has called upon you,

you'll come with a sigh and go with a smile,
too- ra lye-o, too-ra lye aye,
though many, the mile and long is the day,
too- ra lye-o, too-ra lye aye.

CHAPTER 26

Once further south, as Daniel and Emily made their way to Abigail's, Emily could see the outskirts of the Brolen Region just through the trees at the edge of the Berkshires. She looked over as they rode.

"'Twas not afar from here wherefore I was raised and ruled by the nuns. Me thinks I can see the old place in the distance."

"When were you brought there?"

"I know not? I was told 'twas long ago by my parents. Upon question the nuns would answer as such: 'why Emily, thou art seven.' Or two years on - as such: 'Tsk tsk. Remember before you question, Emily. Thou art nine; and lucky to know such, as some here do not even know of their age.' 'Tis something I have pondered at times. Perhaps, it would give me some knowing that the nuns withheld. I did not ask of't at leave, as all I cared of then was to be gone," said Emily.

Daniel brought the horse to a stop and looked at her. "Why not we go? They keep record of such things. 'Tis simple as to enquire."

Emily thought a moment. "Very well than. The place still holds a puissance of unpleasant memory that gives me pause, but I was not, and am not one of those it would breed meekness in." Daniel turned their horse towards the south-west and they made their way to the orphanage. After a time riding along the pathways, they arrived into a clearing where the old building stood. They both dismounted and together entered into a hall and then a rectory where a nun sat behind a counter where shelves of parchment were kept.

She looked up at them and instantly recognized Emily. "Girl. Wouldst thou return? 'Tis not so common."

Emily curtsied to her and did not look down as she used to, but met the sister's eyes. "Sister Maria. I have come to enquire of my admittance records, if I may."

"Admittance records?" She paused. "That you are no longer of our care, they are available as such, within my judgment."

Emily smiled to her. "Thank you sister."

"I did not confer yet."

"Please kind sister," said Daniel.

She looked at them in pause. "I will do favor than."

"My gracious thanks," said Emily.

The sister went to the files and after leafing through them, brought Emily a clipping of papers which she handed to her. Emily looked down at the papers and was in a moment struck by something she saw. Next to the date of her admittance was the name –Anne- crossed out with a line; and to its side was printed Emily. She looked up at the sister with her heart in her throat.

"Prithee. What does this mean?"

The sister looked at it. "'Tis common procedure. If a child arrives and is named as someone already in our care, provided one is young enough, a new name is provided so as to not make for confusion in addressing the children."

Emily looked at her with her thoughts racing, then saw the sole unreadable signature at the bottom.

"Erst while, I were told my mother and father left me here. Is it possible that this were an invention as well?"

The sister looked at her with pity. "Sweet girl. 'Twas long ago. Thou wert brought by a woman, who when asked, told of you being the bearing of forced intimacies betwixt a man and his maidservant."

Emily's head went light and Daniel took hold of her as she faltered and the sister gasped.

"That is enough. I should not have put so much upon the girl," the sister exclaimed, taking back the forms.

Daniel held Emily for support and they walked back outside together where they sat down and talked for a long while.

CHAPTER 27

Sometime later, Abigail was in the sitting room with Sara when she heard a horse approaching. She looked from the window and saw it was Daniel and Emily.

"They've returned," she said with some relief.

She went to the front door, opened it and stood and waited for them as they dismounted and came to her.

Emily ran ahead. "Abigail," she said, and hugged her.

"Dear girl." Abigail stroked her hair.

When she let her go, Abigail looked at Emily and Daniel standing there with curiosity.

"There is some difference with you two. What has come about?" she mused.

Emily took Daniel's hand. "That which was most natural."

"Abigail; we have decided to marry," Daniel said. Abigail looked at them astonished and silent for a moment. "How sudden comes this news. Bequeath me reluctant issue to voice concern herewith, that in silence, would harangue me; and grant my misgivings as quick, yet of this, I must say, doth not the hearts enthrall sometimes play hasty, in a fever at cupids more fickle shot?"

"Thought has been my query to this and else all of days past; and such days these have been, as could not be called haste's lifetime. I have amended and abated these considerations and found them a strange math, as trying to study: a hummingbird in a glass box to see how it behaves: a dragonfly on a string to know its habits. They would suffer and change, stifled of their nature -as I have suffered in my measured analysis. I know I love her, and, who I am as to who she is, is but the hearts logic, which cannot be studied so."

"Than I smile to welcome this joyful news," said Abigail. She held the door open for them and they went inside to talk and rest.

It was some time later that Abigail came to Lewis in the solarium carrying a list. "Lewis. I have a most important errand for thee. Take this list of names and locales and ride forth to deliver these invites. Stress to whomever they are given that the name bearer should receive with promptness; or in lack thereof, a related receiver might leave them most visibly placed."

"I will madam."

"Godspeed."

Abigail then went to the sitting room and looked to the window. She walked over to it and gave a whistle and in a moment, Percy came fluttering down from outside and landed on it there in front of her. She gave him a pet then went to her writing desk where she sat down and began to write a letter. When Abigail had finished writing her letter, the pigeon began to coo and step back and forth at the window sill as though in eagerness. "Alright Percy. Soon enough." Abigail picked up a thin white ribbon that had a small feather lined pouch attached to it. She took her letter and an invite then folded up the pieces of paper and put them into the pouch and went over to the bird. She slipped the light harness onto Percy and the bird started to coo again more loudly and ruffle its feathers on the window sill. Abigail smiled then made two clicks of her tongue this time and the bird shot off in an instant up over the trees, then out of sight.

CHAPTER 28

Melissa arrived home exhausted and climbed the stairs to her room where she fell on her bed and did not move until - not much later; when there was a flutter and beating of wings at her window sill. She looked up with surprise. "Percy," she said with what could be described as excited tiredness. The bird looked at her with a curiosity and amiableness that was enough to muster her to get up and go to him. She carried herself over and gave him a pet, then looked at his pouch with interest, as it seemed to bare a message. "What have you here?" Melissa took out two pieces of paper. She unfolded one that was written in the calligraphy of a formal invite:

You are invited of short notice on the 2nd day of May to the wedding of Daniel Marlett and Emily Harlow outside the estate of Abigail Bellevue in the South Berkshires. The ceremony will commence at mid-morn.

"Harlow," Melissa mused. "Where have I heard that name afore?" She unfolded the second piece of paper which was an additional note from Abigail to her friend.

Dear Melissa.

What a pleasant surprise to discover that you have met two dear friends of mine. I speak of Daniel and Emily. Emily told me of two sweet young ladies named Melissa and Guendoline who sat next her and she had acquainted with at the theatre, and her realization of a known connection betwixt us upon inquiry. They have both told me what a pleasure it was to meet you and that you were the first they informed of their plans to wed. They very much wish you to come as they said you were want to, and thus assured me you were -when they last saw thee- at leave to home with all certainty. We very much desire your presence. Might I ask a favor of you? Afore you commence to the wedding tomorrow, could you make a stop at the jewelers shop? I have commissioned the rings for Daniel and Emily which he has agreed to fashion on such short notice by working throughout the night. I ask this of you, as the shop is quite near your estate and there is much to be done about here. If this is agreeable to you, please send Percy with your confirmation and I shall send him in return, with the jewelers receipt.

With deepest gratitude.

Abigail.

Upon finishing her note, there was a rap at Melissa's door and her father (The Marquess) opened it and entered. "Father."

"Daughter. Where hast thou been all this time?"

"Please, Papa. I will explain thus, but right now, I must rest."

"I will hold you to your word; but very well, my inveterate wanderer. Here has arrived a delivery for thee."

Melissa looked at an arrangement of wild flowers her father held with a perplexed curiosity then took them from him.

"Who from?" said Melissa.

"I know not," said her father. "They were pinned beneath your window this morning whence I saw them whilst out in the garden. If some suitor is to be stealing beneath your window, I should like to know who and have word with him."

"Father. I know not whom."

"Than I will leave you to your notes and such, which will no doubt lead to more outings, I'm sure."

"Not for some time Papa. Not for some time." Her father left the room. Melissa sat down to write back to Abigail:

Dear Abigail,

It would be my pleasure to procure the rings and my delight to attend the wedding of Daniel and Emily. I will keep this short as I must sleep.

Melissa.

Melissa went over to Percy, folded her note and deposited the confirmation message into his pouch. He stepped back and forth and cooed, then with a click of Melissa's tongue, he was gone. After Percy flew off, Melissa fell onto her bed. She had only slept fittingly for the past several nights away and now sighed at the comfort of lying in her own bed. She looked to the window across the room and her thoughts wandered, then became more random and flighty, then hazy as her eyes closed into a deep sleep.

Nemo was on his return journey back to the Berisfurd's estate as it began to grow dark. He often preferred walking to riding as he enjoyed the time and pace for thought and observation. He passed again where he had met Daniel and Emily just a few hours before and smiled at recalling them, then walked further into the Berkshires. After some time, it was getting quite dark and cooling down. Nemo was also getting tired from his outing and decided to stop for a spell. He gathered some branches and sticks and began to build a small fire to warm up and rest his feet for a while. After starting it, he sat against a tree and looked out into the forest. As Nemo sat by the fire, he watched the flames lick up and slowly began to take notice of vague shapes within the trees. He meditated on them, being aware of the disorienting affect a fire can play upon the eyes in the pitch. He imagined a hawk like human figure that held up a finger and traced a line along the cosmos that Nemo followed with his eyes above the tree tops. It melted into the darkness and suddenly there was the ruffle of wings and what appeared to be an owl swooped across the small open area in front of the fire and out into the trees. It startled him somewhat. Nemo relaxed again and looked out through the flames to the forest. He began to make out another shape within the trees. It seemed to observe him. He couldn't see it in detail but it stood on two legs and seemed not quite human; not quite animal. It had a darker, more terrestrial aura. He began to grow fearful and wondered if what he was seeing was real, and just at the moment he did, the ambiguous form seemed to hold out a hand in the darkness. As it dissolved, Nemo had the sudden thought, 'did it wish him to go with it? What should you decide?' Nemo wondered, unsure it seemed, of what he was asking himself. For some time he sat there then when he looked up again, he saw two glowing eyes through the now dying embers of the fire. They fixed on him and seemed to study his thoughts as much as his slightest movement. He abandoned himself to the moment and felt his fear subside into a calmness, then began to think of his life; of certain times and fondnesses, friends and experiences, that seemed to wash over him with a rush of enveloping emotion. Then these thoughts faded out and everything seemed to go quiet. He looked up at the glowing eyes in the dark.

"I'm ready," he said quietly.

In an instant, the wolf bounded out and was upon him and had hold of his neck. Nemo held its soft belly and felt it rise and fall. He felt the animal's hot breath on his neck and face, as it huffed and strained taking deeper hold of him till the blood drained down his neck and he let go of its soft fur and died.

And so the day ended.

CHAPTER 29

The head mistress in the Earl of Bales household whose proper name was Cassy, was very much surprised to receive a wedding invite, as it was a rare occurrence for her indeed (and well timed, because if the earl had been there, she would likely not be able to go.) What was most astonishing to her though was the name upon the invite. She re-read it again very early that morning before setting out on a prior important task.

You are invited of short notice on the 2nd day of May to the wedding of Daniel Marlett and Emily Harlow outside the estate of Abigail Bellevue in the South Berkshires. The ceremony will commence at Mid-morn.

She now felt she had a chance and responsibility to try and right something that had bothered her so long; for in her mind, for many years she had wondered if Jane Harlow knew of the child. Now was her opportunity to find out. Cassy put on her coat and left the earl's estate. She had an idea of where to go, though not an exact address. She went out to the street and began walking as it was only feasible to afford one carriage ride out of her pay, and that would be to the wedding. It was some time later when she arrived on a well to do street in the Anover Region near the North Berkshires, where several estates were situated. Cassy began walking slowly along the boulevard. She had passed this area before on errands. It was here she had one day seen her again, stepping out of a coach with parcels in hand. She walked slowly and glanced casually into the front yards and the windows of the different estates hoping for some opportune glimpse. For some time she did this, walking up and down the street until she thought she might have to abandon her hopes and leave, as the wedding was to take place soon. It was in this tired state of mind that she passed two other maidservants walking past her and overheard their conversation.

"The merchant only had these youngling quails. Jane had wanted something more substantial, but my foot work to another market might have come to a late luncheon, so they will av to do."

"Fret not. Stuff em to the ribs and the knives and forks will keep busy. That's what I do," said the other maid.

Cassy turned around. "Pardon. Ladies, pardon." They stopped and looked to her.
"I could not help but mark your words. I hath need to speak to a woman by the name of Miss Jane Harlow. Is the Jane you spoke of, the same, prithee?"

"'Tis her. Miss Harlow; though I call her Jane."

"Oh dear." Cassy took her invite from her pocket. "If you can favor me a service, I should count myself in yours to any such a thing for the asking."

"What of it?" asked the maid.

"Only to hand her this and bid her meet me at the gates of your employer's estate presently."

The maid looked at the invite with curiosity. "I can do."

"Oh yee are a sweetheart. Thank you, thank you."

"Come than," said the maid as her friend left and Cassy followed her to a near-by estate. She waited outside the gates for Jane Harlow to come.

Many hours later, Melissa opened her eyes slowly and looked around the room then groaned and stretched her arms comfortably. Suddenly her eyes went wide as she glanced out the window. She jumped up out of bed and ran to look at the water-clock across the room.

"Oh, hell. Oh, conundrum. Not now!" She started about unsure of what to do first, then reached for the buttons of her bed clothes; then realized she was not in her bed clothes, having slept in her dress. Melissa put on her shoes and darted to the door and out into the hall -as Percy watched her curiously- then, not a moment later, she returned and looked bemused straight at the bird.

"I know, I know," she said as she walked over and removed his harness then opened his carrying pouch and unfolded a small piece of paper that was the jewelers receipt. "Now. You must stay Percy. Understand. You must remain here." Suddenly Melissa had an idea. She took the bird on her hand then with her other hand, she closed the window and placed it back on the inside sill. "Back shortly," she said then left again and darted downstairs with such speed that her father looked at her across the room dumbfounded where he sat and had tea, fully having expected Melissa to come down and do so as well.

"Not for some time Papa," he repeated cynically to himself as she slammed the door behind her.

A short time later Melissa entered the jewelers shop out of breath. The jeweler came to her and smiled pleasantly.

"Greetings to thee young lady. Might I assist?"

Melissa looked at him and held up a finger to ask him to wait a moment that she could gasp a few times before speaking. He did.

"Rings," said Melissa between breaths. "Two rings for Daniel and Emily." She slid the receipt to him and he looked at it.

"Ah. 'Tis for you. Wondered I when they would be had as they were commissioned to be ready by dawn."

"And had they are, with thanks," said Melissa grabbing the rings from him as he produced them from under the counter in a silk wrap.

Melissa ran from the shop.

"And to thee," said the jeweler though she was already gone.

Melissa's father, while drinking his tea, had heard the sound of something fall upstairs. He got up and went upstairs to investigate. It seemed to have come from Melissa's room. Lord Whitstaff went down the hall to her room and opened the door gingerly. The room was quiet and he thought nothing out of the ordinary, then he saw a small mirror that had fallen on the floor. He went to pick it up and as he did, Percy wandered out from under Melissa's bed then through her bedroom door and into the hall without notice. After he picked up the mirror, Lord Whitstaff went to Melissa's window, threw it open then left, closing her bedroom door and going back downstairs.

Melissa ran back to her father's estate. Her father had sat down again to finish his tea, when she arrived home. She stood in the lobby looking at him with need to catch her breath again before going upstairs. He waited for her to speak.

"Father. Why did not the cock crow of this day?"

"Perhaps he'd been out and about too much as well and overslept."

"Jest. He gives me jest now when there is not a funny place left in my exhausted bones."

"Forsooth; you have exhausted them. Sleep can't catch up with your legs. As to the cock, perhaps than, a fox is somewhere about licking its lips of a tasty answer to that!" he shouted to her as she came to the top of the stairs and slammed her room door with a frustrated huff.

Melissa looked up at the open window of her room with terror. "Father!"

Lord Whitstaff looked up astonished as Melissa came bounding back down the stairs.

"Young lady. Have you come delirious?"

"Father! Why didst thou open my window?"

"Do you honestly require an answer to such a thing? Very well. Air. Air, my dear."

"A bird. Did you see a bird?"

"My sweet. You are starting to worry me."

"In my room father! There was a pigeon in my room."

"A pigeon in your..?"

Suddenly they both looked away as a pigeon fluttered across the ceiling of the lobby and into the sitting room.

"Oh, thank God," Melissa enthused and ran to the sitting room. Her Father now thought she had in fact come delirious.

"Melissa. Sit down and I shall send for the doctor."

"Please father. I need no doctor. I need to catch this pigeon." Melissa whistled and clicked her tongue as Percy darted about the room. After a few moments, the bird calmed down enough that it came to rest on a lamp shade, then looked at Melissa appearing as exhausted as her. It then flew over and landed on her hand.

Melissa walked gingerly from the room and began to go upstairs to her room with Percy.

"Young lady, I need some manner of an explanation!" her father shouted from the bottom of the stairs.

Melissa turned to him from the stairs with the pigeon on her hand. "Just one moment is all I ask. I give you my word. Let me see the bird off and I will."

Melissa went upstairs to her room. "Goodness gracious. What a morning." She took the two rings from her sleeve pocket and deposited them into the carrying pouch then slipped the harness over Percy's neck. She walked over to the window with the bird on her hand. "Okay Percy. It's your turn now." With two clicks of her tongue the bird darted from the window and over the lawn.

CHAPTER 30

It was a bright day outside Abigail's estate. Lewis had set up trellis and lattice work around the yard and arrangements of silk hangings and flowers around the front area where the ceremony was to take place. Among the rows of white wooden seats sat Lidia, Ferdinan, Merchant, Kip, Guendoline, who worried of Melissa and other various peoples and acquaintances.

It was past mid-morn and Abigail decided she could keep the bride and groom waiting no longer. She went inside and to her sleeping chamber, then from a bureau she took out a small jewelry box and opening it, sifted through the small selection of articles that were in there. Abigail rarely wore jewelry and though she had little to choose from, she preferred the option to any other, in view of her relationship to the bride and groom, as well the embarrassing alternative of asking guests for handouts. She was unsure if the ring would fit Emily; and of Daniel, it would be a bare provision at best, for maybe a quarter finger or so. Thus, she was afraid she would have to ask them to try the rings before commencing with the ceremony, though she dreaded to.

Abigail left her chamber and went outside again, as the lute, harp and flute musicians played to the side of the guests. She saw Daniel and Emily waiting to the right and left of the ceremonial alter under separate trellis enclosures. There was something about the way each of them looked at her that said they were ready. The parson raised a look to her as well, and the mood of the crowd was at a pique to begin. It seemed utterly incongruous to detain the scene any longer with a makeshift ring fitting, and with a sudden change of heart, not knowing what it would mean, she nodded to the preacher to begin.

And so the Parson stepped to the front and center of the aisle as the lute, harp and flute musicians brought their song to an end. He looked over the crowd for a moment.

"We are here on this day to witness the joining of Daniel and Emily in sacred union of holy matrimony, before the eyes of God, to share their joy and to celebrate their love. Will the bride and groom step forward, please?"

Emily came forward from under the trellis to the left dressed in an embroidered white dress. She walked slowly then stood at the front of the aisle aglow with happiness.

Daniel then stepped from the trellis to the right and walked to the aisle to join her where they stood together.

"Daniel and Emily, have you come here freely, and without reservation to give yourselves in marriage?"

"I have," each of them answered in turn.

Daniel and Emily looked to each other and Abigail came and stood to the left of Daniel. Abigail was fearing that one of the rings might slip off the brides hand and fall on the ground or not fit on the groom's finger at all. There was nothing else to be done now though, so she tried to put it out of her mind and enjoy the ceremony.

Below the window of Melissa's room were the hedgerows and gardens, and behind them, a small patch of trees. Over these trees were the marble tiles of the Royal Court Square spread outward in all directions for a space of 500 square feet where people walked about. The fountain, as a center piece showered a steady mist around its circumference where Melissa and Guendoline had cooled their feet, and now the swift beating of wings cut through it at a second's time. Outward from the square were many winding pathways; the most southern of which led to two ornate arches which dissolved with swift passage, into a distant background of palace and pathways and marbled square and fountain spread out in a wide perspective view. Trees swayed softly under there foliage as far as the eye could see. Here a lake, there a glade, here a wooden bridge, there a man with a cart, and Percy beat his

wings then tucked them in coasting on a current of wind, no
hindrance or obstacle to a route accented with memory and images,
interaction and sustenance. Above, the thin clouds shifted in shape
as they moved north. Below, some horses veered through the trees
moving south. Between the trees and sky, Percy shot up, then
stooped and bore at a ninety degree angle down into the green
foliage towards a small brown box; which evolved into a stone
structure, which took on details of tower and buttress and glass
dome, then rows of seats, and people standing, and windows in
closer detail.

"Daniel, will you take Emily to be your wife? Will you love her,
comfort her, honor and protect her, and, forsaking all others, be
faithful to her as long as you both shall live?"

"I will."

It was the open window in the middle between the east and
west that the bird maneuvered its wings to touch down upon, but
in that instant it heard a sound it knew as well as any in the forest
and altered direction...

"Emily, will you take Daniel to be your husband? Will you love
him, comfort him, honor and obey him, and, forsaking all others,
be faithful to him as long as you both shall live?"

"I will."

"You may now exchange rings."

Everyone glanced up amazed as a fluttering white bird (that might
well have been a dove) came sailing out of the sky and over the
rows of seats, then with a rush of wind and declining speed, it
landed with spread claws on Abigail's hand as though on cue. With
a quick lithe movement, she opened the pouch and found
somehow what she had hoped she would: two sparkling rings,
which she took while depositing her other ones therein.
Daniel and Emily looked from the bird to her and she handed

the rings to them as they smiled, then Percy flew off to the window sill.

They slid the rings onto each other's fingers.

"I now pronounce you man and wife. You may kiss the bride."

CHAPTER 31

Before the Berisfurds had left for the wedding that morning, Montegue had come to them with a concern. Both of the Berisfurds had wondered at Nemo not having returned, but Montegue had worried, knowing it a possibility that he might have slept in the woods, but most untoward that he would not have returned by morning, especially in consideration of the Berisfurd's plans to attend the wedding; so rather than await word from them on the matter he made a rare decision to go to them and voice his concern. Their minds had been on the wedding that morning. Having this reminder of the issue, they agreed that something must be done and gave Montegue permission to go in search of him. So it was that after the Berisfurds left, Montegue went in search of Nemo.

After the ceremony, Emily and Daniel walked around and greeted the guests. After talking with several people, they came to Guendoline, Merchant, and Kip who were standing together.. Daniel talked with the two men, while Emily took Guendoline aside.

"Guendoline. Dost thou knowest what happened with Melissa?"

"No. We had considered meeting up and coming together. I wish we had as perhaps this could have been prevented, for as appearances suggest, I think she might have...umh, overslept."

"I am not so sure; as this beautiful display of the bird making delivery of the rings, I think, may have been orchestrated by her and Abigail. Honestly. I don't know how they timed it so perfectly. I just hate to think she stayed at home just to perform the task, though it was a very pretty touch to the proceedings."

"You may be right," mused Guendoline, then she looked across the yard. "Oh goodness. She comes as we speak."

Emily looked as well to where Melissa was approaching on horseback. She dismounted at the stable and walked over to them.

"Dear Emily. I am so sorry for my lateness."

Emily hugged her. "Oh. You are a sweetheart. To do such a thing for me and Daniel. 'Twas a beautiful gesture."

Melissa looked at her confused, then a thought came to her.

"Oh. Percy, it is - you speak of. Did he arrive on time, prithee?"

"Exactly on time." Emily smiled then Melissa did too.

"I am so happy for you both," said Melissa.

"Now, you and Guendoline enjoy the proceedings, whilst Daniel and I greet the rest of the guests."

"We will," said Melissa. Emily continued on.

"At least it was a pretty white lie," mused Melissa to Guendoline.

"Very so," said Guendoline.

"Such a morning," sighed Melissa, "and there as well: a bouquet of flowers beneath my window from a suitor I met at my friend Mariel's. Honestly I did not expect it of him."

"Are you quite sure of that?"

"Yes. He is more for casual banter and sometimes crude jests."

"No. Are you quite sure of the suitor. For notice how hither, our young Kip looks upon you fittingly."

"Kip? You must be... It can't be."

"You did encourage at the tavern."

"That harmless bit of flirting."

"Melissa. What you consider harmless flirting, hath played with many a boy's and man's hearts."

"I do not have to try so hard."

"Oh no. I should say, you do it quite easily it appears."

Melissa looked at Kip and smiled.

"Oh; he is as good as smitten. There is something keen about him, that I think him not the doting doe eyed sort though, that would let himself be lead about by the ear till his heart becomes soft-colored, as that one a few fort-weeks hence who left thee flowers at each turning of the clock, and sighed when you would tie your shoe."

"Nor do I. Let us join young Kip and his friends than."

"Let's."

Emily who continued on to greet her guests, saw her former headmistress (Cassy) who was standing with another woman. She smiled and waved to Emily and she went over.

"How glad I am you could come," said Emily "I sent you invite with expectation that you might not be able to."

"He (Your father) is away upon travel of the continents. His brother who is looking to us, is more allowing. I cannot tell you how struck I was, upon reading the name upon the invite. So; it is you? Though you are Emily now. Emily – Harlow?"

"He is not my father, regardless of any evidence to the contrary; and yes. 'Tis I."

The woman who was standing with the headmistress looked at Emily with emotion and put her hand to her mouth.

Emily looked at her thoughtfully. "Miss Cassy. Who is your friend?"

Cassy curtsied to Emily. "I would not be so bold as to bring an uninvited guest to a wedding without good reason. It took me some work to find her, but I did. I should let you two alone." Cassy walked away.

The woman smiled to Emily and looked at her face with utmost engagement. "You must forgive me. Thine cheekbone might be my mirror."

"And thine eyes hast some element as to mine, as though one were fashioned under the other's star," said Emily.

"As did I notice; with desire that we might see thus together."

"Is it you? Are you my Mother?"

"'Tis I."

Emily looked at her wonderingly for a moment. "Why didst not you keep me, if he would not?"

"Keep you? My child. Thy birth brought me to delirium.

Whence I came around I was told you had died. Though I cried to see you, he said 'twas too late and your body had been taken. There is no way to describe how it feels to have a child, brought back as it were, from the dead. To have such a long hopeless pain be swept away in an instant and to be here with you. It is as life in rare occurrences comes fashioned in the stuff of dreams and I have been blessed to experience such a time."
Emily hugged her.

CHAPTER 32

After the ceremony and celebrations, the wedding guests were ready to depart home. Many of them had carriages waiting on the main pathway through the Berkshires to the northern regions. Everyone who had not departed on horseback decided to walk together to the main path and then go their ways.

The wedding guests all left together and walked through the forest in one long line making their way along the smaller trails. At the back of this line was the parson who tended to walk more slowly. It was a few miles in while many were talking and making merry when the Parson felt a hand on his shoulder and stopped. He turned and faced an unfamiliar man who bowed his head to him.

"Thou man of God. May I humbly request your services?"
"What is it my brother?"
Montegue spoke quietly. "My friend and dear companion has been mauled to death by a wild beast just thither of here, and that you might perform a simple right for him; I would be most grateful."
Suddenly The Berisfurds turned and noticed the parson had fallen behind. They saw Montegue with him and went to them.
"My Sir and Missus. Please do not be detained. I did but come to here whence upon my task I did see this procession of people

and the parson at its tail end. I have found my dear friend in death. I wish not to cast shadow on this joyous occasion, but only to have the parson perform a simple right."

"And what would you think, that you would have us pass in ignorance to the plight of one who is as dear to us as to you. Is a marriage a shun for the day to aught but smiles and toasts? That is a natural face for such a day, but should it, in knowing of such a loss, take leave; 'twould be a shame to such smiles. Therefore take us with thee and the preacher or be not in our charge."

"This way than," said Montegue.

As they began to leave, several more people turned and noticed them till at last Daniel and Emily at the front of the line did so as well and came to see what had come about.

"What comes of this?" asked Daniel.

"Dear bride and groom. A sad occasion has come about for us and we must take leave to pay our respects. Please forgive and continue on," said Lidia.

"What is this occasion?" asked Emily.

"A man in our employ. One Nemo, hast been mauled to death by a wild beast nearby."

"Doth he wear a cap stuck with a hen's feather?" inquired Daniel.

"That is he," said Montegue.

"Why. I have seen him twice of recent, and the most goodly of fellows he was. He did smile to me in his coming whilst I was in shooting practice and sing for me in my going upon meeting him hereabouts."

"And I, he did greet and give assist of direction and advice when I were lost, thence I did take the pleasure of his song as well."

"We of must, will not leave until we have paid our respects as well to him and this is how it shall be," said Daniel.

"Come than all," said Montegue and the long procession followed him into the small glade where Nemo lay against a tree, his body now covered in green garlands and flowers.

The Parson walked over and blessed him then all stood about. "Here lies a man of good renown, who finds kind word even among those who knew him not by name. He was a man of thoughtfulness, merriment and song who took pride in his work and felt a strong kinship with the beasts of the earth, though it were one that would take his very life. From the earth we come and to the earth we shall go. May our friend Nemo, rest in peace, for he will be remembered."

The guests bowed their heads in respect then departed slowly back into the forest.

CHAPTER 33

All who had been at the wedding returned to whence they had come and there was a quiet in the Berkshires. Daniel and Emily were at last together in their home. Abigail walked about her solarium and thought to herself that it might soon be time to tell Daniel of some things. Lidia had gone to find solace of Nemo's death with her lover Andrew and realized her marriage could not last. Francis was at his loft painting a face he'd seen while under the influence, Guendoline went home, then went to purchase a flute, Merchant went to prepare the theatres next production, and Melissa went to a park in the court with Kip.

Montegue, meanwhile stayed with the parson and he and some other guests dug a grave for Nemo's body. Felix wandered about the the halls and howled much of the day, then lay inconsolable. Ferdinan prepared his rifle for a wolf hunt the next morning then called Felix, to no avail. Jane Harlow was the last to leave Emily and Daniel after they had showed her their home so that she would know where to visit. They discussed some future prospects for her, while she was walking back to her employ as happy as she'd ever been, and Percy was - somewhere about.

Made in the USA
Charleston, SC
16 July 2016